S0-ASN-123

Stonewall Inn Mysteries
Michael Denneny, General Editor

By Mark Richard Zubro

A Simple Suburban Murder
Why Isn't Becky Twitchell Dead?
The Only Good Priest

The Only Good Priest

Mark Richard Zubro

St. Martin's Press
New York

THE ONLY GOOD PRIEST. Copyright © 1991 by Mark Richard Zubro. All rights reserved. Printed in the United States of America. No part of this book may be used or reproduced in any manner whatsoever without written permission except in the case of brief quotations embodied in critical articles or reviews. For information, address St. Martin's Press, 175 Fifth Avenue, New York, N.Y. 10010.

Designed by Dawn Niles

Library of Congress Cataloging-in-Publication Data

Zubro, Mark Richard.
    The only good priest / Mark Richard Zubro.
        p.   cm.
        ISBN 0-312-07054-3 (pbk.)
    I. Title.
PS3576.U225055   1991
813'.54—dc20   91-15559
                                                   CIP

First Paperback Edition: March 1992
10 9 8 7 6 5 4 3 2 1

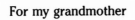

For my grandmother

◢◣ Acknowledgments ◢◣

I wish to thank the following for their kind assistance: Carrie Barnett, Steve Engles, Tonia Gurnea, Diane Mears-Mustafa, Paul Varnell, Allan Wardell, and especially Kathy Pakieser-Reed, Peg Panzer, and Rick Paul.

The
Only
Good
Priest

1

After carefully hanging his clothes in the closet and dumping his dirty laundry into a pile in the basement, Scott sprawled his six-foot-four-inch frame onto the couch, spread his legs far apart, and planted his feet on the edge of the oak coffee table. He shut his eyes and said, "I don't want to be disturbed for a thousand years. Not for nothing or nobody."

Scott wore faded blue jeans, white gym socks, and a University of Arizona T-shirt. He'd just returned from a week-long series of speaking engagements on the West Coast. As the highest-paid pitcher in professional baseball, he gets huge numbers of requests to speak each year.

He opened one eye. "Unless we have chocolate chocolate-chip ice cream in the freezer."

I said, "If we do, you will bestir yourself enough to race like mad to get some before it's all gone?"

"I'd share. Probably."

I sat on the coffee table next to his right leg. I let my finger trace a wandering line from his ankle, around his instep, and then halfway up his leg. "How about hot sex instead. The kind men dream about happening once in their lives."

He opened both eyes and looked at me accusingly. "Tom, you ate all the ice cream."

"I had no choice. While you were gone, alien beings landed in

1

the backyard and demanded the most valuable ransom I could pay."

"That's what you said last time."

"It is?"

"I think you may be fibbing."

"Me?"

Suddenly he swung his legs around and grabbed me, and moments later I rested in a complicated head lock, half under him. He tried to grab several vulnerable parts of my anatomy. I wrestled with his heavily muscled 190-pound frame.

"You caught me by surprise." I laughed and tipped him over. We tumbled to the floor. Instantly we jumped to our feet, circling each other warily.

I sidestepped his next lunge.

We grappled momentarily. He slipped. I slid and he was behind me, arms around my chest and stomach, attempting a bear hug. I felt his chin on my shoulder, his bristly cheek against my neck.

We faced the picture window. I watched a car turn and enter the driveway. "There's somebody coming," I said.

"You won't get out of this that easily," he said.

"Seriously. A car's coming up the driveway." He relaxed his grip a moment to look. I dashed away.

"You rat," he said.

I pointed outside. A huge black Buick slowly maneuvered up the fifty-foot drive. "It's a priest with a couple of passengers, I think."

"Somebody soliciting donations?" Scott asked.

"You don't send priests out on Saturday afternoons in black Buicks to make door-to-door pleas for cash." I tried to see what the priest looked like or to catch a glimpse of the passengers, but they moved up the driveway out of view.

Moments later the doorbell rang. We hurried to answer.

Of the people who stood on my porch I recognized only one, Neil Spirakos, one of the reigning queens of Chicago gaydom.

I live in a farmhouse in the middle of one of the last cornfields in southwestern Cook County. The subdivisions creep closer every year. Soon I'll want to sell. I like the quiet. A visit to the suburbs by Neil Spirakos was a major event.

Within minutes five of us sat in my living room. As Neil explained the reason for their visit, I observed our guests. Neil had stuffed his overweight body into a rocking chair. He wore designer jeans, inappropriately tight on the contours of his lower torso, along with a brightly checked turtleneck sweater that clung to his rolls of fat.

Scott and I sat on the couch. In the wing chair on my left sat a pale and sweating priest dressed in black except for his Roman collar, which he tugged at in sporadic bursts. Moments before, I'd shaken his cold, flabby hand: Father David Larkin. Every few minutes during our conversation he'd pull out a comb and run it through his rapidly thinning hair. No matter how many times he did it, he couldn't cover the fact that the remaining long strands wouldn't be sufficient for long to keep his pate hidden.

In the wing chair to the right sat an elegantly dressed woman with dark hair and fair, pale skin. I have a fashion sense just above that of a learning-disabled snail, but even I could tell without looking at the labels that she got her clothes from exclusive boutiques in New York, Paris, and Rome, plus whatever doodads she picked up on Oak Street in Chicago. Taking off a red coat with black collar and matching black leather gloves, she'd revealed a red knit dress and a black scarf with swirls of spidery red in it draped around her throat. A pair of black leather boots and a small black shoulder purse completed the outfit. From this last she extracted a silver cigarette case and a cigarette holder. On her, this wasn't an affectation. She carried it off with grace and humor. Her sultry "May I?" and lifted eyebrow sent me for an ashtray. I am not one of those radicals who refuses to permit smoking in my house or presence. In my pre-Scott days I liked kissing a man with the smell of cigarettes on his breath.

Neil had introduced the woman as Monica Verlaine. I knew

her by reputation as one of the richest women in Chicago, owner of a chain of gay newspapers in large cities across the country. The most visible, prominent, and powerful lesbian in America.

"Murder," Neil said, finishing the explanation he'd begun five minutes earlier.

The priest pulled out a gleaming white hanky and mopped his upper lip and the fold of his double chin. "I don't believe someone would kill him," he said.

Monica took a short drag from her cigarette, dipped an ash into the nearby ashtray, and watched Neil placidly.

"You have proof for that charge?" I said to Neil.

Neil slammed his fist on the rocker arm. It creaked dangerously in response. "No. The fucking police and the fucking Catholic Church pulled a fast one."

"Please," the priest said.

"Sorry for the language, Father," Neil said. He neither sounded nor looked contrite.

The priest leaned forward in his chair and waved away the apology. "We have no proof it was murder. And while I would never defy or accuse my superiors, there is a moral obligation for the truth to come out." He subsided. Out came the comb.

With cool aplomb Monica reduced Neil's overly dramatic explanation to the basics. She told us that Father Victor Sebastian, fifty-one years old, had been found dead in the sacristy half an hour after the Sunday evening Faith Mass. The police had been called. Chancery officials had shown up. Father Victor Sebastian had been involved in Faith since 1972, when it began sponsoring a mass in Chicago for gay Catholics.

Faith used to be the main gay Catholic organization. I knew they'd had rough times in recent years—internal dissension and fights with the Vatican—but I knew little of the politics of the situation.

Monica explained. "Father Sebastian always spoke for moderation and conciliation. Yet each time the group took a more radical stance, he came with us. When we split up, we didn't

4

think he'd stay." She described him as kind, gentle, and unassuming.

"One of the few actually goddam Christian people in the fucking Catholic Church." Neil said this with no apology to the priest. "Some bastard killed the only good priest in the whole fucking diocese." Another smack on the rocker arm. I winced.

Monica continued the explanation. What little inside information they'd managed to obtain led them to believe the police had done only a perfunctory check. Barely looked for fingerprints, just took a few pictures. The paper said it was a heart attack. "I finally managed to get through to a source in the chancery this morning. He wouldn't talk except to say he'd never seen so many auxiliary bishops and priests scurrying about at all hours. He knew it was a cover-up of some kind."

All three nodded. They each expressed varying degrees of agreement with this notion.

"That doesn't mean murder," Monica said, "but it makes me suspicious."

"Why a cover-up?" I asked.

Neil exploded. "It's like the fucking Inquisition. Those medieval shitheads want to look pristine and pure. They're afraid of 'scandalizing the faithful.' Every time they fuck up, they trot out the 'scandalizing the faithful' bullshit. It's like Nixon, Ollie North, and National Security. Only totally blind fools believe that shit."

Neil is my closest gay friend in the city. For years we worked together on committees to get the Gay Rights ordinance passed. Over the years, he and Scott have moved from barely tolerating each other to peaceful coexistence. Neil hasn't gotten over being picked last for teams in school forty years ago. Scott's being both a Major League baseball player and gay offended Neil's sense of order in the universe. Given Neil's radicalism, I've never understood his attachment to the Roman Catholic Church.

Monica said, "Our friend is dead. We want to know why. He

was in perfect health. We talked last week. I'd never seen him happier or more vibrant."

Scott asked, "If he was such a good guy, who'd want him dead?"

They looked at him in silence.

I added, "What I don't get is why you're telling all this to us."

"He was the parish priest here in River's Edge," Father Larkin said.

I looked expectant.

"You knew that?" Neil said.

I shrugged. "I don't read the local papers very often, and it's not something I would notice. I haven't seen a gay newspaper in a couple weeks."

"You have contacts in the police department here," Neil said.

This was true. For years as a teacher at Grover Cleveland High School in River's Edge, I'd had the slowest classes of seniors and sophomores for English. Dealing with them had brought me into contact with cops, judges, juvenile officers, social workers—the usual paraphernalia of teenagers versus the world.

"You know the system," Neil went on. "You can talk to these people and find out the truth."

I shook my head. "Even if that were true, it happened in Chicago. They'd have little on it here."

"The Church and the cops can't cover up a murder, can they?" Scott asked.

Neil looked disdainful. "In Chicago anything's possible."

Monica said, "We want the truth to come out."

"I really don't see how I can help," I said.

"You could talk to people," Neil said. "People trust Tom Mason, confide in you. We have contacts. You could see them." He nodded toward Scott. "Plus, Scott Carpenter's name can open doors closed to many others."

"You want us to look into this priest's death?"

They nodded.

"No way. Why don't you?"

The priest spoke. "We're too directly involved. We're all known in gay Catholic circles. They'd be suspicious of us immediately."

"And whether you choose to believe it, Tom, you're one of the few gay activists in the Chicago area who is trusted by all factions," Neil added.

I said to Monica, "Your source in the chancery would be in a better position to investigate than we would. Have that person do it."

"He can't. His position is precarious. I was lucky to get out of him as much as I did. I promised not to push him any further."

We argued for a while. They left frustrated, but they extracted a promise that I'd at least think about it.

By the time they left it was after six. Scott and I worked out for an hour in my basement. I've got some old weights down here. At his penthouse on Lake Shore Drive Scott has a complete set of exercise machines. I can still fit into the gym clothes I wore when I played sports in high school and college, and Scott is in great shape by profession, so working out together is a turn-on for us.

The basement is usually cool, but the January thaw outdoors made it warm enough to linger. After half an hour, I lay back on the weight bench dripping sweat, feet flat on the floor. I eased the weights onto the slots above me and drew a deep breath. I heard his weights clank to the floor. I glanced over. He strolled to the bench, eying me from head to athletic shoes. In a swift move he swung a leg over and stood spread-eagled above me. He slowly sat down, his ass resting finally on my hips. I traced a finger under the top quarter inch of his Bike jockstrap. . . .

An hour later, after quick showers, we ordered pizza delivered from Aurelio's in Frankfort and discussed the afternoon's visit over dinner. We agreed there was no point in our doing any kind of investigating. "That's what police are for," Scott pointed out.

We also talked about negotiations at school. I'm on the union negotiating committee at the high school. We'd been meeting with the school board since last spring. January in the Midwest is not the brightest time to call a strike, but it seemed a definite possibility at this point. Nobody wanted to budge, and the teachers were angrier than I'd ever seen them.

The other main topic for discussion was Scott's parents' visit this coming Saturday. His revelation nearly a year ago that he was gay had hit them hard. A reconciliation had taken place, but, as part of it, Scott had insisted they come to Chicago and meet me. We both had some apprehensions as the day drew closer. Meeting one's in-laws for the first time can be delicate.

Around eight-thirty we settled down to watch *Field of Dreams*. I'd gotten him the video for his birthday. We both love the movie. We sprawled on the couch, our feet up on the coffee table, a bowl of popcorn between us.

Neither of us cooks much, witness the pizza for dinner. He took a cooking course a few months ago. Big deal. All it means is when he makes the popcorn, he doesn't burn it anymore. Although to be fair he could make an occasional fabulous holiday feast even before he took the class.

After devouring the popcorn, I moved the bowl to the floor and snuggled, settling into a nice, quiet Saturday night. An hour into the movie, headlights pulled into the driveway. "That better not be the dynamic trio again," I said.

"Maybe it's Kevin Costner wanting to do a threeway."

"In your dreams," I said.

It turned out to be my brother Glen and his oldest boy, Jerry. Of all my three brothers and sister, I'm closest to Glen, who's four years younger. Many Saturday nights he and his wife, Jeannette, stop by, and the four of us spend long happy hours together. Usually we play games. Monopoly is my specialty. Of my nephews and nieces, I'm closest to Jerry. Glen started bringing him on Saturday nights a couple of years ago. I love the kid, but he wins at Monopoly far more than a twelve-year-old should.

They didn't usually stop by unannounced, but it wasn't unheard of. Jeannette wasn't with them. Glen said they'd been in the area and Jerry'd remembered he'd left his hockey skates here last weekend. They planned to stop only a minute.

Glen has the darkest hair of all of us and, at six feet, is the shortest, but he's probably the best athlete. Being youngest had taught him he'd have to fight twice as hard to beat the rest of us. He also has a wicked sense of humor. It cost him a trip to the doctor and ten stitches when he glued all the pages of our older brother Brian's secret stack of *Playboy* magazines together. Brian's got a mean temper.

Glen didn't take off his coat. He sat on the edge of a chair while Jerry searched. We chatted about the Bears' collapse during the past season. Ten minutes later Jerry's voice drifted up from the basement, asking if I'd come help him look.

Glen yelled for him to hurry. I shook off my lethargy and lumbered down the stairs. I found Jerry sitting on the workout bench tossing an old baseball between his hands. He'd only turned on the light for the stairs, so basement shadows drifted from corners and crevices. He gave me a brief smile, all braces. He resembled his dad more than any of his brothers and sisters, especially the way his right ear was slightly higher than the left. I wondered if his peers teased him about it, the way we teased his dad when we were kids. A tough fighter, an honest kid, not a whiner, wearing a junior high-school letterman's jacket a shade too big for him. When he lost a game, it was always, Let's try again. He caught on fast to tricks and strategies.

I sat on the second step from the bottom. Other than the brief glance with the smile, he wouldn't look at me. Tossed the ball back and forth.

"Not here for your skates?"

He shook his head.

I leaned back, resting an elbow on the fourth step. He'd confided a number of secrets to me in the past. Kid stuff, mostly, but I'd always taken him seriously and never betrayed his confidence. Obviously he'd come over to talk. I only needed to wait. In a few years he'd be talking to his buddies, not an adult. For now he was still enough the trusting kid to try me first.

"Must be serious," I said.

He nodded.

"Trouble at home?"

He shook his head.

I walked over and sat down next to him on the bench. It surprised me for a second, sitting next to him, to realize how tall he'd gotten. Hair as dark as his dad's; he'd probably pass him by a few inches in height. I reached over and took the ball from him.

"I'll help if I can," I said.

I met the level gaze of his blue eyes. He gulped and said, "You know, Uncle Tom, how you said you and Scott would never live in fear just because you're gay?"

My turn to nod. "You afraid of something? Somebody bothering you?" I asked this quietly. The dim basement light lent itself to confidences.

He gave a brief shiver in the coolness. "I can't tell my dad. You know how upset he gets." Older brother Brian isn't the only one in the family with a temper. I have the longest fuse of any of them, but when I explode it's probably the worst of all.

"The priest at church." Jerry gulped. "He told me he'd kill me if I ever told."

2

Jerry, I knew, served as an altar boy at St. Joseph's Parish in River's Edge. Glen had married a Catholic and agreed to bring up the kids in her religion. Their religious orientation didn't bother me.

I watched Jerry carefully as he told me the story. He'd served Saturday morning Mass earlier today for Father Clarence Rogers. Jerry had actually forgotten his ice skates in the altar boys' robing room off the sacristy and had gone back to get them. He'd been rooting around in the back of a walk-in closet under a pile of old cassocks when he'd heard angry voices.

Jerry'd only recognized Father Clarence's voice, and he didn't hear everything they said, but a lot of what he did hear was about Father Sebastian. The two voices blamed each other for his death, one of them saying they were lucky to be Catholic priests in Cook County, where people still respected the clergy enough to know when to shut up. They'd yelled about screwing their stories up when they talked to the police.

Jerry'd frozen when the voices started. You weren't supposed to be in the sacristy without permission. The voices faded. Jerry began to think he was safe. He stretched to relax his tense muscles. In doing so he bumped a row of empty hangers. They clanged resoundingly. He prayed the voices had gone far enough not to hear, and for tense moments nothing happened.

Then the door swung open. Father Clarence dragged him out of the closet and raged at him for ten minutes about being a sneak, and a cheat who would go to hell.

"I kind of believed the threats, and kind of not. He was really mad, and he did scare me. Uncle Tom, I don't understand all this." Jerry scratched the brush-cut side of his head. The hair on top and in back flowed in waves nearly to his shoulders. "He said if I told, I'd be sorry. I lied and told him I didn't hear anything, but I don't know if he believed me.

"I thought about it as I walked home. I know I'm not supposed to tell lies, especially to a priest, but I'm glad I did. If I listened to him, I'd have to live in fear. You told me you'd never do that. I won't either." He looked proud, young shoulders squared, chin thrust forward just like his dad's when daring us to fight thirty years ago.

I said, "You were right to tell me. Don't worry about the lie you told him. You don't have to be afraid of some priest. His threats sound like those of a terrified man, not somebody who's practicing what a good priest is supposed to do."

I watched some of the tension drain from his body. "I'm glad I told you. My dad would have yelled and carried on. He might not even believe me. Do you?"

"Yes."

"You won't tell my dad, will you, Uncle Tom?"

"Not unless you say it's okay," I said. I asked him a few questions about what he'd heard, but he only remembered what he'd already told me. I asked him about Father Sebastian. He frowned. Said he didn't know him well. Father Clarence ran the altar boy program and taught them religion classes at school. He'd only served mass for Father Sebastian twice. They'd barely talked before and after the service.

"What are you going to do?" Jerry asked.

"What do you want me to do?"

He looked at me carefully, then gave me a wicked grin. "Get the son of a bitch."

12

"I think I'll have a little chat with Father Clarence in the morning."

"Don't hurt him too much," Jerry said.

I smiled. "I won't." I clapped Jerry on the shoulder and stood up. "Maybe I'll beat you at Monopoly tonight," I said as we mounted the stairs.

I won the last Monopoly game. First Glen, then Jerry, landed on Marvin Gardens with a hotel just after I made a fortunate deal with Scott. Served them right for bankrupting me in the first two games. They left at eleven.

I've got an old VCR and a small TV in the bedroom. We threw the unfinished movie into the system, turned the sound on low, got undressed, and crawled into bed. Scott sat up with his back propped by a mound of pillows against the headboard. I pressed my back onto his chest. He draped his arms around me. He waited until we were comfortable to ask what was bothering Jerry.

I pressed the pause button on the remote control.

"How did you know he was upset?"

I felt him shrug. "Instinct."

Scott is great with kids, especially those under six years old. When we'd known each other about two years, I agreed to baby-sit Glen's kids while he and Jeannette took a two-week cruise to the Bahamas over Christmas vacation. I half expected Scott to retreat to his Lake Shore Drive penthouse, a recent purchase after his first million-dollar contract. Instead, he'd eagerly volunteered to help. Some things I'm good at. They don't include little kids, but I owed Glen and Jeannette a big favor.

Jerry'd just turned five. The other kids were younger, down to six months old. Over the two weeks we'd done a couple of family things with my other nephews and nieces: Lincoln Park Zoo, the Field Museum. Scott amazed me. He can organize a herd of unruly kids as well as any mother. Then, after a mildly chaotic, kid-filled New Year's Eve, Jerry woke up in the middle of the night frightened, crying, and throwing up. I hadn't the first notion of what was wrong or what to do. The kid wouldn't stop being sick. I'd about decided on a trip to the hospital emergency room when Scott padded into the kitchen. Through his yawns he quickly sized up the situation. He took the kid, and I ran to get dressed.

Minutes later I found them in the rocking chair in the darkened living room. I watched from the kitchen doorway. Scott rocked Jerry slowly, speaking softly to him. The crying had become intermittent. Once in a while Jerry asked for something to drink.

I brought a glass of water from the kitchen, knelt next to them, and offered him the drink. Scott shook his head. "He won't keep it down," he said. "Bring me a towel."

I dashed to the bathroom and hurried back. "What's wrong with him?" I whispered.

At that moment Jerry let out a series of plaintive cries. Scott soothed him. "He's probably got a touch of the flu. He shouldn't drink anything until he's done throwing up. When that's over, we could give him a few sips of warm Coke."

Of course there wasn't any in the house. So I ran to the White Hen at 191st and Wolf Road. I got back in ten minutes. The two still rocked. Jerry was crying softly and whining, but his arms were tightly and trustingly entwined around Scott's neck.

"Let's try a little of the Coke. I think he's had time for his stomach to settle enough." I opened it and gave it to him. The kid kept it down. The crying bouts came farther apart and the sips closer together. Some time before he sent me back to bed, Scott told me he'd learned his kid skills taking care of his older sister's family as he grew up. He spent most of his teenage years either playing baseball or baby-sitting.

Later, when I felt him crawl into bed, I glanced at the clock, saw it was five. He'd been up over three hours.

"Jerry okay?" I mumbled.

"Fine." He sighed.

I snuggled close to him. I knew then—if I'd ever doubted

it—that I loved him and wanted to stay with him forever. Later I told him. Fortunately, he felt the same.

Now I filled him in on Jerry's story. His reaction was the same as mine: we had to check it out. I outlined my ideas for the next day. Besides a visit to the priest and the cops, I wanted to see Neil and his buddies. I'd find out if this Father Clarence committed murder, and if he did, I'd nail his ass to the altar. Nobody threatens my favorite nephew! When Jerry told me, I'd masked my anger for his sake, but while telling the story to Scott, I'd begun to get furious at this priest. Scott calmed me down, and we discussed strategy for meeting the priest the next day.

Around midnight we turned the movie back on. We wound up engrossed in Kevin Costner building his dream. We cried at the end as we always do. I clicked off the TV. Scott nestled into my arms, and we fell asleep.

Next morning I woke Neil Spirakos at 9 A.M. He cursed at the interruption of his beauty sleep, which even he acknowledged he needed more than the rest of us, but stopped when I told him I'd changed my mind about checking into the murder and explained about Jerry. I told him I wanted to meet with the people in the Faith organization who had the closest connection to Father Sebastian. He promised to set up a meeting for some time that day. They had a board meeting at four and Mass at six.

I phoned the River's Edge police station and asked Frank Murphy if we could see him. A police lieutenant and an old friend, he agreed to meet us late that morning.

I tried calling the rectory but only got an answering machine. It said their office hours were Monday through Friday nine to eleven-thirty, two to four, and seven to nine. I'd never heard of part-time clergy before. I figured if you wanted to be a priest, it was sort of like being a doctor. People's troubles don't usually come conveniently according to fixed schedules. Maybe I'm old-fashioned, but if you're in the business of helping people with problems, aren't you on duty twenty-four hours a day?

We decided to drive over and confront Father Clarence unannounced. We arrived at St. Joseph's Church to a slowly emptying parking lot. Caught in the traffic as we inched toward a parking spot, I had time to read a prominently displayed historical marker. The plaque boasted that the structure in front of us had been built with the earnings of the good farmers and first burghers of River's Edge. Since this is the oldest southwest suburb of Chicago, after Blue Island, the church was well over a hundred years old. The faithful had kept it in pretty good repair. The original red brick, aged to a depressing maroon, enclosed a stolid rectangle broken only by narrow strips of stained glass that crawled two stories up the side of the building. There used to be a steeple, but it had burned three years ago; the firemen were just able to save the church itself. An ultra-modern complex sprawled around the old building: a school of gleaming new bricks, a gymnasium complex, a rectory that was obviously somebody's idea of a modest $500,000 suburban bungalow.

"I thought these Catholic Church guys were supposed to help poor people, not live in luxury," Scott said. "This looks like something a TV evangelist might build."

"Don't be prejudiced," I said. "I don't think it makes a lot of difference which denomination they are. The clergy's pretty much the same all over."

"I guess," Scott said.

Several parishioners pointed us toward the sacristy at the back of the church. We entered a well-lit stairway that led up. As we climbed, a door banged open. Seconds later two giggling fourteen-year-olds tumbled by us. We heard the door below burst open, then crash shut. At the top of the stairs was a room filled with cabinets, benches, desks, cupboards, and cubbyholes, all made of wine-dark mahogany. A stained-glass window let in daylight. A muffled voice called that he'd be with us in a minute. The only light came from the window, a few lighted candles, and a doorway through which I could see an altar surrounded by mounds of fresh flowers—a large expense, I thought, in cold January.

A smiling young man emerged from the closet. His face clouded when he saw us. "I'm Father Clarence. May I help you gentlemen?"

Model-handsome, his black suit emphasizing his leanness, this was a man who would turn the heads of both men and women as he walked down a street.

"New to the parish?" Father Clarence said, striding purposefully toward us, hand outstretched. He pointed to Scott. "You look familiar."

I introduced us as Jerry's uncles and explained our concern about what Jerry had said. He responded with words of wounded innocence and calm reason. The bastard almost pulled it off. Maybe he went to suave school. The old ladies of the parish must eat up his act. They'd want to mother him, and let it show, and secretly want to pinch his youthful ass, but hide that deeply. Yet he'd escaped the effeminacy so often associated with priests and ministers. Men would like him. He'd play baseball and drink beer with them. I almost missed the oily shiftiness in his eyes. Without seventeen years of teaching school and ferreting out teenage lies from truth, I'd probably have been fooled too.

He denied everything Jerry said. Claimed the boy'd been troubled for some time. Thought of talking to his mother about changes in the boy, a new moodiness. He didn't like to bring it up, but perhaps a few signs of drug abuse? He tossed this last statement off casually.

I think his smugness infuriated me the most. That and his calling Jerry a liar. Scott recognized the signs of my rising anger and stepped between us. He rarely loses his temper. The media call him "the iceman" for his cool under pressure.

"Look, buddy," he said. "We're going to check out everything we can about Father Sebastian's death. You've called Jerry a liar. Kids do lie. In this case, I don't think he did. When I find out the truth, and if you're implicated . . ." He paused and gave the icy stare that had paralyzed more than one Major League batter. "If you're implicated," he repeated quietly, "we'll be back."

Father Clarence kept his mouth shut but left a pitying smile on his face.

All the way to the meeting with Frank Murphy, I swore at the priest, defamed the Roman Catholic Church, and cursed all self-satisfied hypocrites.

For the police station, the January thaw had proved an unfortunate event. The deeper the snow got, the more it tended to mask the flaws in the crumbling debris-encircled structure. Dirty, faded bricks, possibly once yellow, crept around a two-story disaster area. Gutters lay stacked and dented against the side of the building. They'd managed to pay for the things but forgot to allocate enough money for someone to finish the job installing them. In the autumn someone had raked leaves, rusted beer cans, and broken glass into huge piles now revealed by the retreating snow. In a vain attempt to dress up the place in the past year, someone had smeared orange paint over the building's battered old shutters. Unfortunately, the town's landmark committee now wanted the place preserved as a historical site. Because of this, for the moment, they could neither fix it up nor tear it down. They certainly didn't have the money for a new station.

Inside, the officer on duty wore a bright blue uniform shirt, crisply ironed, along with a congenial smile on his face, presenting a pleasant contrast to the grimy walls and nicked and scratched counter.

We met Frank in an interrogation room. It contained a table, three chairs, four walls, and a door—all painted flat gray. A rusting radiator hissed at us softly.

Frank wore a conservative blue sport coat, black jeans, white shirt, and a loosened red tie. He greeted us warmly.

He and I had had some great successes and some equally spectacular failures with some very messed-up kids over the years. Last June we attended the college graduation of a kid who spent what was supposed to be his senior year in high school in Stateville prison. We'd managed a miracle turnaround on that one. It's good to remember those kids when month after month you stand by helplessly as others toss away whole lifetimes.

We talked awhile about the coming baseball season and then about troubled kids. Frank and I had to make a court appearance in a couple of weeks in a parental custody battle. Neither one wanted the child.

I asked about Father Sebastian, explaining my interest.

He shook his head. "We're only peripherally involved. He lived here, but he died in Chicago. It was a nothing case. Thousands of people die like him every day. Too much cholesterol and they keel over. Fifty-one's not too young for that."

I told him about Monica's perception of his health and spirits.

"She a doctor?" he asked.

"No," I said.

"Do I need to say more?"

I grimaced.

He continued. "I'm not saying your nephew lied. You and I have both heard more fantastic stories from kids less trustworthy that turned out to be horribly true. But look at what we've got: a twelve-year-old kid versus a popular priest." He held out his hands palm up and shrugged. "Who wins?"

I sighed.

"I know all the priests over at St. Joseph's. My wife and kids go every Sunday. I show up if I'm not working." He gave us his impression of the priests in the parish. He continued the litany of kindness and light we'd heard for Father Sebastian: a good man in the right sense, willing to help, go out of his way for anybody for the smallest thing. Father Clarence he didn't care for. "I agree with your judgment. Something about that guy is wrong. He's too perfect. Does everything right. Kisses the asses of all the right parishioners. Lots of people began to ignore Father Sebastian, talked about retiring him. Poor guy, doing a

19

simple good job, and this flashy kid steps in." He shrugged. "It happens."

"You think there was jealousy?"

"Nah. Sebastian didn't work that way, and if Clarence felt it, he'd never let it show. Although . . ." He hesitated. He eyed us carefully, stretched his legs out, and crossed them at the ankles. "I hate to repeat tawdry gossip."

We leaned forward.

"I found this out from the guys on the night shift." He cleared his throat theatrically. "Father Clarence isn't always where he belongs."

"Huh?" we said.

He explained. On nighttime emergencies involving parishioners needing a priest—for last rites, for example—because the rectory had an answering machine, someone, usually the police, wound up banging on the rectory door. Several times Father Sebastian had let it slip that it was Father Clarence's night on duty. Father Clarence drove a very expensive red Corvette that Frank's source claimed often didn't appear in the rectory parking lot until just before 6 A.M.

"Where does he go?" I mused aloud.

"None of our business generally," Frank said. "He could have a sick mother in a nursing home, or maybe he's getting a little nooky on the side."

"I thought priests weren't supposed to have sex," Scott said.

"They're human," Frank said, "no matter what the Vatican tries to tell us."

He agreed to do some discreet checking into Father Sebastian's death but didn't promise anything.

At home there was a message from Neil on the answering machine to get back to him. I called, and he said we could meet with the Faith board of directors at five and then Neil wanted to see us himself. Scott spent the afternoon responding to letters from AIDS groups around the country asking him for help with fund-raisers. These are his priority now. As a star athlete he draws huge crowds, and he always appears free for AIDS groups. I spent the afternoon reading *The Company We Keep* by Wayne C. Booth.

I drove Scott's Porsche to the city. I guess it's juvenile, but I love its power and sexiness. My new gleaming black pickup with oversized tires and four-wheel drive has a certain sexual cachet, but his car is magic. For the forty-five-minute trip to Chicago, we took I-80 to I-57, up the Dan Ryan Expressway, and then over to Lake Shore Drive. The board met in an upstairs former dance studio on Clark Street, across from the Organic Theater. Fortunately, enough snow had melted so we found a parking space in less than fifteen minutes.

Upstairs, we entered a room that ran the length of the building. A large cluster of over a hundred metal folding chairs filled the half of the room closest to the windows overlooking Clark Street. A simple table draped with a white cloth waited for the congregation in a clear space in front of the chairs. The other three walls, including the back of the doorway, still had the floor-to-ceiling mirrors of its dance-studio days.

Neil got up and came over from the circle of people sitting in the far corner. His pink-and-purple-checked sweater vest hung over his paunch. It covered his faded blue-jeans shirt and the top third of his tentlike pants.

"You're just in time. We just finished," he said. He glanced around quickly at the group at the far end of the room, then whispered, "I've got to talk to you after this!" Everything is a crisis with Neil. His having to talk to us could concern something as simple as a hangnail or as heavy as a nuclear disaster. As he led us up to the group, he said, "I'll introduce you; then you can ask questions." Five people besides Neil sat in the circle. We pulled up folding chairs and joined them.

Neil introduced us. To my left sat Monica Verlaine, whom we already knew, dressed today in a black wool skirt, a red wool form-fitting jacket with black buttons down the front, black silk scarf splashed with red and white draped over the right shoulder of the suit jacket, black earrings, low-heeled suede boots, and matching purse. No cigarette holder or smoking for now.

Next to Monica sat a man in his seventies, at least, bald and smiling: Bartholomew Northridge, former accountant and treasurer of the organization. His hands shook sporadically. Every few minutes he'd hold them together in rigid stillness, only to have them wander apart moments later to shake again. He spent much of his time darting nervous glances at other members of the group.

Then came Father Larkin, who nodded pontifically.

I knew the next person from a bar we frequented: Prentice Dowalski, twenty-three or -four, part-time bartender and hustler, willowy thin, strikingly handsome face, smart-mouthed, who generally hid behind a string of rude or stupid comments. Several years ago I'd accidentally learned that Neil occasionally pimped for Prentice. This was only for exceptionally high-class clients who paid over $1,000 an hour. I couldn't imagine what a hustler could do to earn that much an hour. Then again, maybe I didn't really want to know. I hadn't been around him for long enough stretches of time to know if his stupidity was congenital or an act. He and a Chicago cop used to be lovers, but they'd broken up a year ago over the hustling issue.

Between Prentice and Neil sat Brian Clayton: short hair and mustache, a hint of a paunch, desperate to look thirty while rapidly approaching forty. Secretary and chairman of the membership committee, he smiled warmly and fussed over Scott and his fame.

Neil cut him off. "We've agreed that we think somebody killed Father Sebastian, and we want Tom and Scott here to look into it." Heads nodded. Neil continued, "We knew Father Sebastian best. Our insights might guide them to the truth."

"What we need to know," I said, "is the type of man you think Father Sebastian was, what you remember from that last day, if you noticed anything different in him lately, and where each of you were at the time of the murder."

Their memories of the last day coincided fairly well. During the board meeting the week before, Father Sebastian had seemed as placid and calm as ever. Mass had been the usual. No one had noticed anything alarming or different in Father Sebastian's sermon that Sunday.

After the service, the group had a social hour. Father Sebastian had gone downstairs to the sacristy, really more of a storage room for the group's files and paraphernalia. That's where they'd found his body. Except for Clayton, who found him, no one admitted leaving the dance room we sat in, but each would be hard pressed to prove their continued presence there. During social hour people mingled, formed groups, and dispersed as at any party.

"So any of the people present could be a suspect, which was how many?"

"Eighty-six," Clayton said. "I always keep accurate count and seek out any new members to make them feel welcome, encourage them to join formally."

"Anybody new this week?" I asked.

No strangers had shown up. It'd been a day of ice, snow, and rain just before the current thaw. The inclement weather kept the size of the group down.

I pointed out the impossibility of our questioning all those people with no official sanction. A collective look of helplessness was followed by silence. In the mirrors I watched them shift uncomfortably.

Neil spoke. "I know it's tough, but our friend is dead. We have to do *something.*"

"Besides the police explanation of natural death and the possibility of someone at the Mass killing Father Sebastian, there's always the stranger or tramp from the street solution," I said. They fell silent.

"What the hell is this?" a voice snarled from the door. I turned to see a woman in a bright-red vinyl jacket, tight Levi's jeans, and white high-top basketball sneakers advancing toward us.

Neil introduced her as Priscilla Kapustaglova, President of

Faith Chicago. He explained why we were there, adding what Jerry had told us. "We think they can help," he finished.

She snorted. "A macho two-bit jock and a schoolteacher?" Hair unkempt, anorexically thin, no makeup, and what I suspected as a perpetual sneer on her lips, she straddled her chair backward like a Western movie extra. "You don't want much from a couple of amateurs."

"They're our best hope. Tom Mason is trusted everywhere in the gay community. If he asks questions, people will take to him," Clayton said.

Priscilla pointed to Brian. "You're drooling because you think they're hot men." Clayton turned slightly red. Priscilla continued. "Father Sebastian died. The cops questioned us. They said it was natural causes. No conspiracy. No murder."

"I wouldn't expect you to trust the cops." Bartholomew alternately clutched the back of his head and twined his fingers together as he spoke.

"At least, one of them was a woman," she snapped. "And yes, I trust the cops in this. I wouldn't trust the fucking Cardinal if he swore on a stack of cathedrals. But a female cop? Sure."

"Naïve."

Monica uttered the one word, and Priscilla became slightly quieter but no less hostile. She asked, "Why was this decision made without me present?"

Neil spoke quickly. "You had another meeting today. This was urgent."

After ten more minutes of squabbling, they declared a truce in their internal politics.

After we got the Father-Sebastian-was-a-saint litany, even from Priscilla, she said, "See? Nobody had a reason to kill him. Give up. Go home."

"Not yet," I said.

We talked about Sebastian's mental state. More serene than ever was the consensus; nothing else different.

"Did he have a lover?" Scott asked.

"He took his commitment to celibacy very seriously," Bartholomew said. He joined his hands together. "He always took time to chat with me after each Mass. He visited me each week. I live alone. I don't go out much. But every Wednesday he came and spent a half hour. I appreciated it. He told me he hadn't had a relationship since before he became a priest." General hesitant nods at this.

"He was gay?" Scott asked.

"Of course," Neil said.

Prentice spoke up. "I do know he met some guy every Sunday night at Roscoe's. I don't know if he was a lover or not, but I saw them once in the back on the couch looking secretive."

Roscoe's was one of the more popular gay bars in the city. Beyond seeing them, and drawing a possibly erroneous conclusion about their behavior, Prentice knew no more. It was something to check out later.

Other than these people, Father Sebastian had no close friends in the group. He met with them. Never had a fight with them, or with any member of Faith Chicago. They'd never heard him exchange a harsh word with anyone.

For the last ten minutes, stray group members had begun filling the space near the door, standing uncertainly, occasionally gawking at us.

The rest of our questions earned no further information. A few minutes later, as the others began moving away, I said to Monica, "We'll have to talk to your source in the chancery."

She looked disconcerted. "I'll try to arrange it, but I don't think he'll agree to see you."

The board of directors moved to their routines, places, and customs with the gathering crowd. I heard a few whispers of "Isn't that Scott what's-his-name?" as Neil led us down the stairs. We examined the storage closet, sacristy, office. We saw vestments, chalices, prayer books, crosses, and winebottles, all cluttered, jumbled, and cheerless, especially after a week of cops and Christians mucking about.

Back upstairs we grabbed our coats and were ready to leave. I reminded Neil about his wanting to talk privately.

Neil searched our eyes and glanced behind him at the rapidly filling chairs. "Fuck this church shit. Let's get out."

We walked up Clark to Belmont and over to Ann Sather's Restaurant. Tonight it was a little less crowded than usual, and we managed to find a quiet corner where Scott could be pretty much out of the sight line of possible fans.

When Scott's no-hitters in games five and seven of the World Series brought the championship to Chicago for the first time in decades, it became difficult for him to be in public without being mobbed. We've been forced to leave restaurant meals unfinished because of the adoring hordes. One oddity is that we're more likely to be forced out of exclusive dining spots by obnoxious patrons than from popular neighborhood restaurants.

After we sat down, Neil started to prattle, but I held up a hand to stop him.

"Neil, I'd give up this whole shitload of trouble right now except for Jerry's being involved. I care a great deal about him. Your group did not impress me."

He began to speak. I stopped him again.

"Do you have any idea of what you're asking?" I repeated the string of possible scenarios, then added. "The guy's a saint. Nobody wants him dead. Everybody's sad he's gone. Priscilla's a creep, but my impression is she'd act like a fool any time and being a fool isn't a sign of murderous intentions. One pretty priest in the suburbs might have his ass in a sling for reasons I can't begin to fathom. It's bullshit."

"Will you listen to me?" Neil asked indignantly.

I nodded.

"You can't give up. I had suspicions before this about the chancery. Now, this suburban priest—what's his name, Clarence—confirms it. Something's up. Besides"—for one of the rare times since I'd known him he looked uncomfortable and evasive—"the whole truth hasn't come out."

3

We placed our order. I eyed Neil suspiciously. "What truth?" I asked.

"Let me tell this my own way," he said.

I shrugged.

He began with gossip about the people we'd just met.

"You've heard of Monica Verlaine by reputation, of course. Her wealth and power go far beyond her gay newspapers. She owns real estate galore in this town. She has a stock portfolio that rivals mine."

Neil's riches started from a nearly bankrupt waste disposal company left to him by a sugar daddy years before, when dark-haired, slender, muscular Neil Spirakos commanded the highest price of any call boy in the city. He'd proved frugal in savings, clever in management, and smart in investment.

I raised an eyebrow about his knowledge. "Monica tells you a lot."

"No. I have the same accountant. He tells me a great deal. He remembers the old days fondly. I still supply him with cute young things as his need arises."

Neil explained that Priscilla Kapustaglova worked for Monica as managing editor of her local paper, the *Gay Tribune*. Priscilla kept the file on lesbian and gay political correctness in the city, reaching almost a gurulike status with the easily impressed.

Neil thought Priscilla must have an ambivalent view of Monica. Probably envious of her money, jealous of her power, but so far desperate enough for a job to keep relatively quiet. Seems Priscilla had no newspaper training but only a year of junior college in Nowhere, Iowa.

"That was a fairly pussy-cat performance for Priscilla earlier," Neil said.

"Why elect her head of Faith?" I asked.

"The woman can organize efficiently with a minimum of bullshit. She'll work harder than any ten people."

I nodded that I understood. I'd worked with far too many gay organizations with the same problem. Two of the fatal flaws of many of these groups were total inefficiency and a tolerance for useless bullshit unrivaled by any but the largest cattle herd on earth. After the passage of the gay civil rights bill in Chicago, I decided it wasn't worth putting up with all the bullshit, so I became less active.

Priscilla had worked for Monica for two years. A number of years before that, Priscilla had shaved her head in protest over lesbians being excluded from power positions in Chicago's gay community. Now there was Monica in what Neil suspected in a position that Priscilla thought was hers by right. Priscilla had struggled for gay and lesbian rights in Chicago from the day she arrived from Iowa fifteen years before. Monica established headquarters here two years ago and coopted all power and attention. At first Priscilla jumped on the bandwagon, thinking that lesbian power had arrived. Unwilling to admit she'd confused satisfying her ego with attaining power, and facing thirty, never having held a job longer than five months, she now rattled about the *Gay Tribune* office, monitoring whatever it was that politically correct people waste their time monitoring. Neil said Priscilla had been involved in a failed lesbian newspaper just before Monica stepped in with her money. He suspected a bailout or buy-out. He'd heard rumors of personal and corporate bankruptcy on Priscilla's part.

Neil said, "She's mixed up in that group, Lesbian Radicals from Hell."

"That can't be their real name," I said.

"No. It's the usual officious crap of humorless radicals. Maybe it's Lesbians for Freedom in the Face of Oppression by Evil Non-Women. Who remembers?"

Neil began dunking one of the cinnamon rolls in his coffee. He took a bite, then continued. "I hate her. I knew Priscilla had another meeting today. It should have gone on until we were done. I hoped she wouldn't show up at all. Her performance today was really rather mild. Of course, Monica does step in, but that doesn't always work."

Neil seemed somewhat in awe of Monica, although I suspected this might be simply envy at her riches. According to Neil, both women had liked Father Sebastian. Priscilla viewed him as the closest thing to a politically correct male she knew, and it tickled her fancy to find him in the paternal Roman Catholic Church. And the priest had responded to Monica's dignity. Neil guessed they shared an upper-class background. He couldn't picture either woman with the slightest motive for murdering Sebastian.

Father Larkin constantly worried that his work with the Faith group would get him in trouble with the Cardinal. After the Cardinal threw the Faith group out of the Catholic Church, they usually had had to go outside the diocese to get priests to serve the community. Sebastian stuck with the group and didn't worry about it. They'd imported Larkin from Milwaukee; Neil often wished he'd go back and stay there. The man pontificated at the drop of a moral issue. He thought Sebastian had tolerated the man, but could report no animosity.

"Why import priests?" Scott asked.

Neil sighed but paused before he spoke, swallowing, I suspected, most of a dumb jock crack. "Don't you read the papers?" He knew Scott'd graduated from the University of Arizona with a degree in engineering, but Neil had a college prestige streak in him. Less than an Ivy League certificate and you were suspect. My M.A. in English from the University of Chicago was barely acceptable.

"I don't pay much attention to the gay Catholic stuff myself," I said.

"You have no excuse," Neil said.

"I promise if I ever get to pick teams, I'll chose you first," Scott said. This crack, I suspected, got to the heart of some very basic resentments. Neil had been a willowy wimp in his teen years. From what he'd told me I knew the slights of his youth still rankled.

Forestalling an eruption of hostilities, I got Neil involved in explaining. In late 1986 something called the Congregation for the Doctrine of Faith sent out a letter supposedly approved by the Pope and signed by a Cardinal Ratzinger. Neil turned an ugly shade of purple, his voice steadily rising, fist banging the table, as he explained each point. "The homophobic bastards declared gays intrinsically evil and homosexuality an objective disorder, and they blamed us for our troubles because we stood up for our rights."

"Who cares what the Catholic Church thinks?" Scott asked.

Neil stared at Scott open-mouthed. "Some people think God is important in their lives."

"Yeah, but the Catholic Church? Who can take a church seriously that declares some man to be infallible. He's just some guy."

"The Pope is not just some guy. And he's only infallible in faith and morals," Neil corrected.

"I don't care if he's only infallible in balls and strikes. He's just a guy," Scott reiterated.

"I wouldn't expect you to understand." Pity for a poor, ignorant jock dripped from Neil's voice.

"I'm not the one going to hell for my sexuality," Scott retorted.

Touché, I thought, but I didn't want to hear them bicker. I wanted data. "What happened after the letter?" I asked.

Neil told the story. Bishops around the country started

throwing gay groups out of their churches. In spring 1988, events came to a head in Chicago. The gay Catholics held meetings—chaotic was Neil's mildest term for them. Tears and recriminations, shouts and threats, compromises and desperate attempts at reconciliation all proved futile. Out they had to go. The Faith group splintered in three. The largest, retaining the Faith name, kept most of the leadership and moved to the old dance studio. They kept close ties to the national organization, which declared—probably heretically, Neil thought—that being gay was okay. The other groups named themselves Hope and Charity.

The Hope group, as far as Neil knew, was still trying to work within the current church structure. The Charity group, smallest of the splinters, had something to do with the Council of Trent and Latin masses. Neil didn't know any more about them beyond that. Personally, he was glad the two groups split off. The people remaining in the Faith group now had a much easier time moving on their political agenda.

He went on. "We even got the chancery to send over their big-deal troubleshooter, Bishop John Smith, to a meeting. I think he came because he and Sebastian were old friends from seminary days. Did no good. Smith was a total arrogant snot, and you know it takes a lot for me to accuse someone of that vice."

"During these meetings," I asked, "did Father Sebastian take sides, lead any fights, make any enemies?"

Neil paused and thought. "Not that I remember. No." He said that Sebastian had sat back, tried to help each speaker clarify his thoughts or express himself, tried to get people to listen to one another.

"What kind of trouble could he get in from the Cardinal by staying with you guys?" I asked.

"Hard to tell. If the Cardinal learned about it, he could get suspended from priestly duties." Neil shrugged. "Sebastian never seemed to worry about it."

"Are all priests gay?" Scott asked.

"All the ones I know are," Neil said. "It's an extremely closeted homophobic society. The most closeted ones being the most homophobic." Neil harrumphed and returned to describing his fellow board members.

Bartholomew was exactly as he seemed: a lonely old man terrified of offending anyone, especially Priscilla. Neil hadn't known of the weekly visits from Sebastian, yet found this typical of the priest's kindliness.

Clayton, a new board member, little known to Neil, was given to non sequiturs and drooling over sports heroes.

Prentice we all knew. "I think you should get behind his flighty queen exterior. That boy knows secrets, I can feel it. I didn't know Sebastian met someone secretly."

"I thought you knew all the dirt in town," I said.

"Not like I used to. Plus he's a bartender. They have a network all their own. Besides, I know he went downstairs after Mass before Sebastian died."

"You haven't said anything?"

"No. I saw him only because I was down there too." Now he looked sheepish. A first in our relationship.

I demanded an explanation.

"Every Sunday I went to confession after Mass."

I gaped at him.

He drew himself to full queenly erectness in his chair, almost knocking over the tray of desserts the waitress was offering him. He chose his dessert, a double helping of chocolate cream pie, looked at us, looked at it, and proceeded to devour it before he spoke. "I will not be called to account even by you, Tom Mason, dear friend that you are, and I know you don't really want to know my lists of sins, unfortunately far fewer than they once were." The point was that he'd gone down, confessed, and left a smiling Sebastian. On his way back up the stairs, Neil had passed Prentice going down. He hadn't noticed Prentice return.

I asked why he hadn't mentioned this before. Too ashamed to tell in front of the group, he claimed. That sounded lame to me after knowing him all these years. He answered by reiterating that he knew of no reason any of them had to kill Father Sebastian, including Prentice. He didn't want to make public accusations in a group still emotionally upset by all the recent changes and divisions.

"Did Sebastian ever talk about this Father Clarence guy?" I asked.

"Nope. He seldom talked about himself, much less anyone else."

I repeated that I wanted to talk to Monica's source in the chancery. If we could break through the church silence, I was sure we'd find out what, if anything, had happened in the basement of that dance studio. He said he'd try his best.

Before leaving, Neil told us Prentice had the nine-to-two shift that night at Bruce's Halfway There Bar. We might stop in and talk to him about his trip downstairs.

We decided to drop the car at Scott's and walk to Bruce's, a couple of blocks down North Avenue just past Wells Street in a building that looked as if it'd been put up the day after the Chicago Fire. On the way, Scott asked about Catholics and confession. I explained as best I could for someone raised in a vaguely Protestant home, but who'd grown up in a heavily Catholic suburb. He shook his head. Reared Southern Baptist and knowing few Catholics as he grew up, he found it foreign.

"I don't see Neil doing something like that," Scott said.

"Belief makes people do weird things, I guess," was my only comment.

Bruce's Halfway There Bar is a very discreet, high-class bar. It used to be the only gay bar Scott would go to, for fear of being exposed as gay. Now he'd enter any of them, as long as he didn't have to put up with obnoxious gay fans who wanted to know the secret sex lives of all major league baseball players. I've never asked. I'm only interested in *our* sex life.

It was a quiet Sunday night, with all of six patrons, four of them seated at least three stools apart at the long bar that ran the length of the left-hand wall as you walked in. Two sat in the

33

front booth discreetly holding hands under the table, knees touching, sixty years old apiece if a day, eyes only for each other, very much in love, it looked to me.

After getting a couple of Watney's on draft from Prentice and asking him to join us when he got a minute, we checked into the back booth. A semicircular affair with high-backed walls, it offered all the privacy a frightened closet case could want. I liked it because it would ensure privacy in our interview. One company must make the cushions for all such booths. Otherwise, how could all the seats be the same dull red color mixed with a multitude of matching rips and tears in the fabric?

As occasional hairdresser, bartender, and hustler, Prentice Dowalski lived one of the more unconventional lives I knew of. Whimsy and chance seemed to be his ruling passions. On a given night he might turn down a thousand-dollar hunk of a trick for some little old man who'd saved for a year to pay fifty dollars for half an hour. Prentice talked about his two arrests as if they were a lark, claiming he'd seduced two or three cops each time.

Instead of lifting the partition and walking over to us, Prentice hopped to the top of the bar, twirled his legs over and around, and jumped down. He'd changed clothes from church. Now his pants clung tightly to his ass, hips, and legs, clearly outlining his dick and balls. The modified muscle shirt emphasized thinness rather than muscularity. Thin combined with cute can cover a multitude of sins.

We got breezy greetings and slaps on the back. He sat with his right arm draped around Scott's shoulders, body intimately pressed close, left hand disappearing under the table.

Scott gave him a mild look. "Sorry, I'm taken, and if you don't move your hand in two seconds, it'll come back broken."

Prentice whooped with laughter, moved a discreet six inches to his left, and folded his hands primly on top of the table. His tenor voice existed just this side of an annoying whine.

"You guys are so *married.* I bet you've never cheated on each other."

Nine years we've been together. At the beginning we promised each other we'd be faithful. I never have cheated. Neither has he, or I'd like to think I'd know if he had. Now, of course, any sane gay couple didn't cheat, or had to cheat so very, very carefully it was hardly worth it.

As a hustler Prentice had told us numerous times quite sanctimoniously how careful he was to do only safe sex. I hoped for his sake he wasn't giving two guys in their late thirties a line he thought they wanted to hear.

"Sad about Father Sebastian," I said.

"A great old guy. I'll miss him. I mentioned I sold my body for a living to that other priest, that Larkin guy. I thought he'd have a stroke. Didn't faze Sebastian. Asked me if I made a good living and if I was happy. Never brought it up unless I did first. Neat guy."

I asked if he agreed with the older people's idea that there was something strange about Father Sebastian's death.

"Yep, sure, they're real adults. Stuff like that's important to them."

He returned to the bar to fix a round of drinks and did his jump, twirl, and hop routine coming and going over the bar. Youthful energy can be nauseating at times.

"What'd you go down to see Father Sebastian about last Sunday?" I asked.

He tried feigning confusion, threw in a little indignation, and settled into a pout. "Who says they saw me?"

I gazed at him levelly. He turned to Scott, whose blue eyes have bored through tougher defense mechanisms than Prentice ever dreamed of. Mine in particular. Scott stared calmly. Prentice gave a guilty gulp and said, "Okay, so I went to talk to him."

"About what?"

Prentice evinced a pronounced stutter as he blushed and squirmed out his explanation. He'd been talking every week for some months with Father Sebastian about going to confession. His chosen profession provided the major obstacle. Prentice wanted to make a real confession. As he put it, "A get-into-heaven no-strings-attached deal." Father Sebastian sympathized, but he wanted a commitment about quitting or at least cutting back on the hustling. He himself had no special problem with Prentice's job, but he thought the church and God might. Prentice saw the logic in that idea and agreed to meet with Father Sebastian each week, at least to talk over his sins, working up to a confession. Prentice had gone down to set a time for later that night. He claimed he left the priest humming quietly.

He looked at me head down, eyes and lashes raised à la Lauren Bacall. The effect was less than enchanting. He couldn't pull it off. I couldn't picture him going to confession either, but I didn't detect any lie in his voice. Maybe the kid wanted to get out of the life. Maybe he'd found someone who'd listen to him and take him seriously as something beyond a sex object.

"There is one thing I should add." He smirked.

I encouraged him with a nod.

That night he'd seen Bartholomew enter the john, heard the old guy cough and spit. The john was a four-by-four cubicle across the hall from the sacristy. When there weren't a lot of people or noise you could hear men's or women's piss hit the water. Prentice reported this last with great relish.

So at least three of them had made unadmitted forays to the basement a short time before Father Sebastian's death. With the john so close, any number of people could have come down and used it.

Prentice interrupted my reverie. "What you really want is the totally deep dish I know on all the board members."

I raised an eyebrow.

He did the round of drinks routine and returned. "You're ruining business." He pointed discreetly to a well-dressed elderly gentleman alone at the bar. "You're looking at a thousand-dollar trick," he said.

"Talk," I commanded.

Mainly he knew about Priscilla and Monica. The younger

woman had made a play for the older. Monica'd rejected her, none too gently. According to Prentice's source, whom he wouldn't name, Priscilla still had the hots for her. "I think it must be Monica's tits."

I gave him a questioning look.

"They're huge," he informed me.

I hadn't noticed. I don't pay attention to a woman's endowments. Now, a guy's crotch I can talk about fold by crease. There's nothing like a hot basket, tight ass, broad shoulders, and solid stomach muscles.

He continued. "Anyway, just recently dear Priscilla got pitched from an all-woman's commune apartment house after only three weeks." Prentice heard they'd got fed up with her more-politically-correct-than-thou attitude and ditched her. Monica let her live in the back half of the third floor of the house they used to put the newspaper together. Prentice had been to Monica's mansion, too, actually three houses on Wellington Avenue between Broadway and Clark that she'd bought and had renovated into one huge place. "Furniture to die for. Each room better than a showroom. Class from floor to ceiling. Ten-foot Art Deco sconces from Vienna flanked the front door. The main fireplace was faced with bird's-eye maple applied in a grid." He went on to describe numerous other examples of chic elegance. He'd taken a number of the gentlemen he entertained to parties there, explored every crevice, and promised himself he'd have the same someday.

Several new customers came in. He swung over to serve them.

The last of the newcomers proved to be Brian Clayton. He spotted us and hurried over.

"Neil said I might catch you here," he said.

We invited him to join us. He grabbed a Heineken and sat down next to Scott. He dithered a few moments, being the shy fan, but Scott's used to that and put him at ease. They talked curve balls and strikeouts for several minutes. Brian had a great deal of advice on how to pitch to certain hitters. Scott bore it all with equanimity. He'd gone through that before.

Prentice saw Brian and didn't rejoin us. Brian said, "I wanted to talk to you guys. Partly because of Scott. I still can't believe you're gay. Are there other—"

Scott cut him off. "Sorry. I've never asked how many gay athletes there are, and I don't care."

"Sorry. Curious, is all."

Scott nodded noncommittally.

Brian also wanted to talk murder. After a wary glance to see that Prentice was at the other end of the bar and couldn't hear, he said, "I'm not in with the other board members. They're real cliqueish. A bunch of my buddies got together. We wanted somebody on the board from those of us who were newer so we wouldn't be ignored anymore." This was one of the reasons he paid close attention to new members each time. He wanted to get to them before the other faction did. Eventually he and his group wanted to vote the others out. Seems Neil had ignored them, and they were totally fed up with Priscilla. I could picture Neil freezing them out. The old A-list gay syndrome from years back lurked very near and dear to Neil's heart. The old queen considered class and custom the cornerstones of western civilization.

"That Priscilla's a bitch." Clayton continued, listing her many sins and slights. "I never knew so many ways a person could be rude. At one meeting I counted her nasty comments: none directed at Monica of course, four at me, three at Neil, eight at poor Bartholomew, six at Larkin, two at Prentice, none at Sebastian."

He never saw any of them socially. Bartholomew and Prentice followed the lead of the others in treating him as an outcast. He resented it. He explained that he told us all this because he had knowledge of their movements that Sunday. "I want you to know I'm prejudiced against these people from the start, so you can judge fairly when you hear what I have to say."

I gave a nod of encouragement.

He took a sip of his beer, wrapped his hands around the green bottle, and looked again to see where Prentice was. Leaning closer and continuing in a whisper, he told us that after Mass on Sunday a week ago he'd been waiting for his lover, Arnie, whose parents were in town, making him late for church. He'd watched the door continuously in anticipation of his imminent arrival. He emphasized this several times. Then, after Father Sebastian had gone down to change, all six of the others had at one point or another gone downstairs, Priscilla being the last, before Brian himself. No one else from the congregation had descended. None of them knew he'd been watching.

When he'd gone downstairs to go to the washroom, he'd heard noises in the sacristy. "I went in and"—he gulped, then continued—"I saw him die. It was terrible." He paused to pull himself together.

"That must have been awful for you," I said, to break the silence.

"Yeah," he said weakly. He took a sip of beer, shuddered, then resumed.

"You seem like okay guys. I think I can trust you. Sometimes with those others it's a fucking zoo. They don't have to be outrageous or obnoxious every minute. Even Monica and that damn cigarette holder are stupid." He didn't know what to do with his knowledge. He didn't want to go to the police. He felt a certain loyalty to protecting his own. He also was afraid the cops might think him stupid or might even suspect him. After our meeting with the whole group, he wanted to talk to us. So when Neil came back and told them we might be going to Bruce's, he decided to stop by.

"How did you get along with Father Sebastian?" I asked.

"He was always good to me. Went out of his way to make me feel welcome. If someone killed him, I'd like to see them caught. I can't believe anybody would murder him."

We chatted with him awhile. A nice enough guy, I guessed. He left.

A wrinkled hand gripped the side of the booth. Moments later the head of another Faith board member, Bartholomew Northridge, peered around the side of the partition.

"May I sit with you?" he asked.

I invited him to join us. He glanced cautiously around the room and fearfully back toward the doorway. Then he tottered over and dropped into the booth alongside Scott with so much force I thought he might break some bones. He licked his lips, coughed, took out his hanky, and spit into it.

"Monica said you'd be asking me questions about Father Sebastian's death." He clutched one quivering hand with the other. "I didn't kill him."

I told him we weren't going to accuse anybody, just find out what happened. I told him he'd been seen and heard downstairs.

His hands began wandering over his body, nervously picking at nonexistent lint, scratching his head, rearranging the wisps of white hair that gathered randomly on top. He began rocking, back and forth in unconscious motion.

"I'm scared," he said.

Gently, I tried to find out of what. He stared at me mutely for the longest time. Finally, his washed-out gray eyes rested on Scott.

"You're famous, aren't you?" he whispered.

Scott nodded.

"When I was young, I was attractive enough to have all the sex I wanted. Now I can barely afford to pay for a little human closeness once a month." A tear glittered in the old man's eyes, rolled down his cheek. He looked at Scott. "May I touch you?" Scott immediately moved closer. Their eyes met and the old man stopped shaking. Gingerly Bartholomew reached a hand out. It landed first on Scott's shoulder. Scott's blue eyes bathed him in warmth. From tentative pats and caresses of his shoulder Bartholomew rubbed his hand over the flannel shirt-covered arm down to the wrist. The angle they sat at in the back of the booth let me catch only glimpses of the next movements of Bartholomew's hands as they moved to Scott's

40

kneecap. Then, with eyes downcast, he moved his hand nervously up Scott's thigh. He renewed the body rocking with his hands inches from the folds of Scott's crotch. My lover didn't flinch. His eyes waited for Bartholomew to look up. With a wrench of courage, the old man brought his eyes up to Scott's. The rocking stopped again.

Bartholomew took several deep breaths. Then the wrinkled hand moved to find the top of Scott's head, patted the soft blond hair. With two fingers he traced Scott's eyebrows, nose, cheeks, left ear, chin; finally the tip of one finger touched each lip. Bartholomew's hand fell away and tears coursed down his cheeks. He cried silently. Scott moved even closer to the old man, put an arm around his shoulder, and hugged him tenderly. No two-year-old clung tighter to Scott's neck than Bartholomew did at that moment. Scott soothed him, murmured kind words, rubbed his back with one hand, held him tight with the other.

After several minutes I heard Bartholomew murmur, "Thank you." They unclinched. Bartholomew pulled out his enormous hanky, yellowed from years of overuse and inadequate bleaching. Scott remained sitting close to him, and after Bartholomew cleaned himself up, Scott put his right arm around his shoulder, took Bartholomew's frail, wrinkled hand, and wrapped it in his own. The old man laid his head back on Scott's shoulder, using it for a head rest.

I explained to Bartholomew about checking each person's story and the need to find the person Sebastian met with each week. He gulped, squeezed Scott's hand, and nodded. He told us he'd gone downstairs to use the john, then stepped over for a few words with Father Sebastian, the only person who took time for him, didn't laugh at him behind his back. He knew he kept the job as Faith's treasurer because Neil secretly checked his books and reports each week.

"I don't need his pity. I'm eighty-two years old, but I know my work." There was a fierce professional pride in his tone.

He told us Father Sebastian was the only one who ever visited him. His parents and sisters died years before and his nephews lived far away, and they'd never been close to begin with.

"Father Sebastian wanted me to get out more. He told me I should volunteer to help people with AIDS. I was scared. I know that's stupid. He told me I was silly. I got mad at him the last time he visited. So I had to go see him Sunday, downstairs. I had to know if he was angry with me. He wasn't. He smiled so nicely. But he told me I had my health, and I should help others, and he'd be taking me to Howard Brown Memorial Clinic this week." He hung his head and squeezed Scott's hand. "I said I couldn't. His kindness made me feel so guilty. I said horrible things, then left as quick as I could." He gulped, but held back the tears. He sat straighter in the chair. "I'm going this week. I'll do whatever I can for them. I've got to make it up to him, and I'll help you boys too."

He grinned for the first time. I saw the gleam of his denture clips. He glanced around the room and leaned forward confidentially.

"Priscilla," he whispered. "I've heard her. She talks violence, destruction, and murder. She threatened Father Sebastian last Sunday before Mass. Threatened to kill him, I don't know why. She scares me. Usually she ignores me, like I'm deaf and slime, but I hear." He tapped his right ear. "I hear perfectly."

He leaned back, perhaps exhausted by this confidence. I thanked him. Whether from lack of knowledge, trust, or energy, he told us no more. We chatted briefly, then walked together to the door. We offered to get the car and drop him someplace, but he refused, insisting he could make it on his own. He and Scott hugged briefly; then the old man disappeared down the street.

We walked back to Scott's. After the bitter cold earlier in the winter, the forty-degree weather in January caused us to linger as if it were seventy in June. I had Monday off in honor of Martin Luther King's birthday, but the next day's schedules dictated two cars so we made the return trip to River's Edge.

We decided to stop by the rectory to see if the good Father Clarence was all snug in his suburban bed. Perhaps we might follow him to the trysting place Frank Murphy had posited. We arrived at the church just after midnight. In the parking lot a red Corvette nestled between two black Chevies. A gray Toyota pickup truck sat three parking spaces away from them. The only light in the rectory shone from the front windows on the first floor.

"Late-night visitors?" Scott said.

"I guess priests can stay up late and party," I said.

We parked halfway down Altadena Terrace, close enough to see who came and went. After fifteen minutes Scott said, "What if the neighbors see us out here and call the police?"

I pointed to the ramshackle, run-down houses around us. "On this side of town they won't notice, of they'll think we're cops."

"In a Porsche?"

"Okay. They'll think were drug dealers, which is even better. They'll know better than to fuck with us."

After half an hour he said, "This is stupid."

I said, "Haven't you ever seen them do surveillance on TV? Before the commercial comes on they always get a lucky break."

He sighed. "We couldn't see anybody's face from back here anyway."

I started the car and moved us a quarter of a block closer.

After forty-five minutes his fidget index hit its limit. "Tell me why this is a sane thing to be doing! It may not be zero outside, but I'm starting to get cold. This isn't summer here." The annoyed thrum at the back of his voice told me I'd better come up with some solid logic quick. He fixed his blue eyes on mine.

"A few more minutes?"

"Fifteen. Solid limit. We leave no matter what."

I shrugged grudging agreement.

Fourteen minutes later the rectory door opened.

"Look." Scott pointed.

Still buttoning his coat, and in nonclerical pants, Clarence hurried across the parking lot to his car.

He tore off down the road. I made the Porsche purr after him. Down 161st Street to Wolf Road, through Mokena, right on Front Street to School House Road, a jog through New Lenox to Laraway Road, over to Route 52, then down to Manhattan. Just inside the little town he turned to the right toward a cluster of two-story apartments houses a block from the highway.

I'd closed the distance significantly on entering town. He parked in the driveway at the first apartment house on the north end of the complex. The door opened before he knocked.

"A sick parishioner?" Scott said.

"Not his parish. I saw a woman in a very short and sexy nightie. I don't think this visit was to bring her communion."

"A girlfriend?"

"Not unheard of."

"For a priest?"

"There's got to be *some* heteroxsexual priests. Then again, I'm not sure." I told him my brother Glen's story about the old priest who performed the wedding ceremony for him and Jeannette. The priest spent most of his time insisting that all the women in the parish loved him.

"Setting up his heterosexual credentials?" Scott asked.

"Sort of. Except Glen said he ruined the whole effect when he spent the entire reception solicitously checking out how much the handsomest young men had drunk."

"Another fag priest," Scott said.

"Probably. Glen said it was embarrassing when the priest tried to be chummy. It was as if the guy thought a sex spy from the chancery might be checking up on him."

The lights in the downstairs apartment flicked off one by one. I doubted if Father Clarence had to worry about his hetero credentials. Barely hidden at the edge of a denuded cornfield, I didn't want to wait for departure. If the Manhattan police stopped to ask questions, we'd be hard pressed to explain our presence.

Back the way we came and home again home. "So he's got a

girlfriend," Scott said as we sat at the light at Gouger Road and Route 30.

I felt sorry for the guy stuck in his vows, no one to hold him in those special times, good or bad. Yet he'd gone into it open-eyed. No one forced him to be a priest, as they had in the Middle Ages.

In the car on the way home Scott turned frisky and rather bawdy, even for a Porsche on darkened back roads. I managed to get us home with most of our clothes on. I made my mistake when I pulled the car onto the darkened side of the house. Love in a Porsche doesn't have a lot to say for it. Even with our athletic acrobatics, discomfort reigned.

We did a serious workout for two hours Monday morning. After showers we had stale Cheerios and milk almost ready to turn sour for breakfast.

"Great meal," Scott commented.

"You didn't have to cook it. I didn't burn it. That equals gourmet around here. Shut up and eat."

He had an eleven o'clock photo session at a cable TV station in Forest Park. He left and I drove to the River's Edge police station. Smack in front of the place sat a police car with four flat tires and a cop sitting behind the wheel staring ahead. He never blinked as I walked past him, up the steps, and into the police station. Inside I asked Frank what that was all about.

He said, "A mistake," and offered no further explanation.

I told him about Father Clarence's nocturnal wanderings. Frank raised an eyebrow and chuckled but said he didn't imagine it had anything to do with Father Sebastian. He didn't want to doubt my nephew, but he hadn't been able to establish any connection between Clarence and Sebastian's death.

"I did find out some strange stuff." We walked to the gray conference room. Today the radiator gave off sporadic clangs. He tipped his chair back, leaned his shoulders and head against the wall, and steepled his fingers. Then he rubbed them along the sides of his nose.

"Good news, bad news, what?" I asked.

"Odd news. Information missing. I had to be very discreet. I tried a courtesy call to the cops in charge of the case. Not the least interested in what I had to say." The cops had sounded bored and put upon but had also evaded every question. Usually the city and suburban cops cooperated fairly closely. Many of them had trained at the Chicago Police Academy together and knew one another from way back. Most little suburbs didn't have the cash or manpower to create an enormously expensive training program for one or two cops. Instead they sent them to Chicago, where they got some of the best training in the country.

"Got nowhere with them," Frank said. "Wouldn't even let me check the files. I backed off quickly. They wanted to know my interest. I stalled them with a bullshit story about suburban cop paperwork. I don't think they bought it."

Then he'd tried the Medical Examiner's office. An old friend worked there. Even this guy hesitated to talk, but finally he said one thing. In putting the files in order at the end of the week, he'd noticed the Father Sebastian report out of place. A quick inspection told him some documents were missing. He checked with a number of co-workers. No one had seen anything.

Frank did his two-handed nose rub again. A few reports remained, mostly lab work that must have arrived after the other materials in the file had been taken. In fact, his friend had gotten the blood report back from the lab just half an hour before Frank called.

"Father Sebastian tested positive for the AIDS antibodies," Frank said. "I guess I never really thought about there being gay priests. Of course I never really think about priests much at all."

"He was sure about the test?"

"Yep."

"That couldn't have been what killed him?"

"Nope, but what did is no longer in the files, if it ever was."

"Your friend make a stink?"

"He reported it to his superior. The woman took the file and said she'd investigate. My friend's worked in Chicago long enough to smell a cover-up. He says this one stinks from Evanston to Gary. 'Some heavy shit is going down' is the way he put it."

I told Frank what I'd learned from the Faith group on Sunday.

"If he took his commitment to celibacy seriously, as they claim, how come he was HIV positive?" Frank asked.

"Could have had a blood transfusion. Or maybe they didn't know him as well as they thought," I said. "I'd like to find the guy Prentice said he met every Sunday."

"Good luck," Frank said. "So far you haven't found anything to indicate Sebastian's death wasn't due to natural causes. I don't think you or I can do anything about the missing file stuff. I can tell you one thing. The initial cop on the case and his partner got called off it within days. That rarely happens. You might try them." He gave me their names.

I left wondering how Sebastian had become HIV positive. Somebody had to be close enough to him to know. Maybe one or more of the six Faith board members had held back information. I wondered if we had enough to pressure Clarence further. And I wanted to talk to the rest of the Faith board about their trysts in the sacristy Sunday.

4

Late that morning I drove to Scott's. I parked my black pickup truck among the BMWs, Cadillacs, and limousines. I greeted Alfred, the doorman, and rode the penthouse elevator up. I spent an hour waiting for Scott in the music room listening to the Minneapolis Concert CD by Ed Tricket, Anne Mayo Muir, and Gordon Bok.

For lunch we grabbed a corned beef sandwich at the corner deli and hurried to an appointment at the *Gay Tribune*. Their office existed in the hot new area of town along the Halsted Street strip between North Avenue and Fullerton.

Inside, chaos reigned. Broken glass from the shattered picture window scrunched underfoot. Plastic and metal computer fragments lay strewn over the landscape. Heaps and drifts of paper continued to cascade as people sifted through them. All the desks sat upright, but the drawers were dumped out onto the floor.

Monica sat on top of a stepladder, cigarette holder clamped in her lips. Youthful male and female underlings scurried about. Occasionally she'd be asked a question. She rarely did more than point. A phone rang and Monica picked a cordless model off the top of an eight-foot bookcase. We heard no part of her conversation. She wore dark blue bib overalls with a pink silk blouse underneath, along with Air Jordan tennis shoes. No matching purse in sight.

A kid who couldn't have been more than fourteen demanded to know what we wanted. She wore orange plastic glasses, baggy pants, a Mohawk haircut, and a paint-spattered T-shirt that said EAT THE WHALES. I asked to talk to Monica. She said, "Mom's too busy. Can't you see we had a break-in? Unless you're cops." She peered at us. "Not ugly enough. Fuck off."

Only twelve feet wide, the room ran the length of the building, maybe fifty feet deep. Monica caught sight of us from her perch halfway down the room. With languid grace but surprising rapidity, she descended the ladder and closed the distance between us. The child stalked off without a word or look passing between them.

"The third-floor office is undamaged," Monica said. "We can talk there." She led the way up narrow stairs. Large holes gaped in the walls as we climbed. She pointed to them. "From the last break-in, not this one."

The glimpse I got of the second floor made the first look pristine. They hadn't started cleaning here. The attackers'd covered the walls and mounds of debris with splotches of white and green paint. If you could cut it, they had. If it was breakable, it was in pieces. She led us into an elegant third-floor office.

"Quadruple-locked and burglar-proof up here," she said. "Because of Priscilla living in back, we put in extra protection. It's on order for downstairs."

Photographs by JEB lined one of the walls. The fourth had a picture window that looked out on Halsted Street. Monica pointed to several indentations in the picture window. "Almost shot up the place a couple of months ago. Fortunately I had them install bulletproof glass when I moved in. You can't be too careful when you're a gay businesswoman. At least I know some stupid kid with his dad's assault rifle can't blow me away."

We stepped around a cantilevered desk crafted of rosewood burl with inlaid zinc zigzags. She seated us in comfortable chairs around a glass-topped coffee table. On the corner of the table nearest to where I sat was the *Cunt Coloring Book* by Tee Corinne, with an open box of Crayolas carefully placed to let the looker observe the cover completely.

"You've had break-ins before?" I asked.

"Twice, although this is the worst. I'm planning to make it the last. And today is deadline. We'll have some computers working soon. The paper will be out on time."

"Who did it?" I asked.

She pulled a cigarette from a cookie jar on top of the coffee table and a silver cigarette holder from a clip on the side. She organized these and lit the cigarette before she answered. "Who knows? Jealous lesbians? Envious gay men? Threatened straights I've put out of business? This is a sideline, a hobby for me, but somebody's going to pay." She spoke very calmly for all her threatening words. Her violet eyes met ours as she puffed contentedly.

"You're here about Sebastian." She didn't wait for confirmation. Her eyes got misty. "He knew people, understood them, not in some saintly, otherworldly way but like a real person, looking at real foibles and major character flaws, and yet he still cared about them. He's the first professionally religious person—priest, minister, nun, whatever—I ever met who was actually a holy person, a good, kind, loving Christian person. And some bastard murdered him." The glint of tears appeared in her eyes.

"How can you be sure it was murder?"

"I know bullshit from cops when I see it. Plus my contact in the chancery is very reliable."

"Like I said last night, we need to talk to your source," I said.

"I'm trying to get him to agree. I'll need more time."

We told her about Sebastian testing positive for HIV antibodies.

"Test can't be right. He didn't have AIDS. I'd know. He couldn't have hidden it from me."

"Maybe he didn't know," Scott said.

"Possible," she conceded. She mushed out her cigarette in an ashtray large enough to hold half of Lake Michigan. She sighed. "You're here because you found out I went downstairs that Sunday." Stated, not asked. "I figured, with you talking to the troops, it'd come out. I am not universally loved." I liked her melodious and soothing voice.

"I went down to talk to him about getting rid of Bartholomew as treasurer. The man is a menace." She recounted a string of the old man's sins as treasurer. "I'm a businesswoman," she finished. "I can't stand incompetence, no matter how kind we should be to the old coot."

Sebastian had refused, saying the old man needed to feel wanted. The group would survive any blunders he made. It wasn't as if Bartholomew were stealing from them. "My last words to him were petty, harsh ones about a totally unimportant issue." She sighed. "Life's a bitch."

After a few moments she continued. "I've never met a more powerful or strong-willed person than Sebastian. Yet he never raised his voice, put himself forward, or joined a faction." She'd neither seen nor heard anyone else making their way to see the priest that day.

I explained about trying to find who Sebastian met at the bar. Who he might be and why Sebastian met him.

Monica thought. Inserted another cigarette in the holder and began puffing. "All I know is that if anybody ever talked about going for a drink, he always suggested Roscoe's. We went a few times. He never met anybody when I was there."

It wasn't much, but that's all she gave us. I got a photograph of Father Sebastian from her. I wanted to show it at Roscoe's: a slim chance, but at least a place to start. Monica had to get back to the paper. She told us she'd send Priscilla up to talk to us. She picked up the phone receiver, punched several buttons, and requested Priscilla's presence.

A few minutes later Priscilla stomped in. She did not sit. She gripped the back of a chair hard enough to turn her knuckles white.

"What is it?" she demanded after Monica left. "I've got work to do."

"Did you know Sebastian tested positive for the AIDS antibodies?" I asked.

"The old bastard had AIDS? I don't believe it. He was so moral. I can't believe he'd ever have sex with anybody. Who'd want to? Still, he was the only politically correct male I knew. Don't know how he pulled that off."

"Why'd you go downstairs to see Sebastian on Sunday?"

The question set her off. For five minutes she berated us as incompetent males and unwanted outsiders. Scott got up and walked to the window halfway through the tirade.

When she paused for breath, I said, "Did you kill him?"

She switched instantly from macho pig insults to deadly calm. "You heard of Lesbians for Freedom and Dignity?"

I nodded.

"We don't put up with insults from men."

"It wasn't an insult, just a question."

She waved a finger in my face. "You'll be sorry, fucker," she said and stomped out of the room, slamming the door behind her.

"I refuse to deal with that shit," Scott said, coming back from the window.

We walked downstairs. The cleaners had reached the second floor by now, but it still looked to be unusable for days. Downstairs, a few computers hummed, repair trucks sat outside, tie-clad men peered into the insides of terminally ill machines. Repair men in hours, that was power and money at work.

We'd promised to pick up Bartholomew at two. He had given us his phone number and address the day before. We called ahead to make sure he was home. No answer. We drove over. Bartholomew lived above a straight bar on Lincoln Avenue, just south of Diversey. No Bartholomew waiting outside, as he promised the day before. We banged on the downstairs door and pressed the buzzer. Still no answer. We tried the first-floor tavern. Behind the bar, a bald little guy with a towel draped over his left shoulder had his bookie receipts spread out on the bar top. A cigarette with a one-inch ash dangled from his lips. I watched him as he deftly moved his beer glass two seconds before the ash dropped. The ash received a swipe with a fist, and the beer returned to its rightful place. "Help youse?" he said, not looking up.

We stood on the other side of the bar, waiting. Finally he looked up at us. He gaped. "Scott Carpenter." His cigarette plopped into his beer. "Whatever you want, it's on the house," he said.

"We're looking for the old man upstairs, Bartholomew Northridge. Know him?"

"You mean the cranky old fruit?"

Scott tapped him gently on his flabby chest. "You mean the kind old gay man," he said softly.

The bartender looked at the finger and smiled weakly. "Yeah, sure, sorry. Who's prejudiced?"

"Have you seen him?" I asked.

"Nope. Should be up there. Most days he stops in here around noon. Not always."

With only a little prodding from sports hero Scott Carpenter, the guy gave us his key. Again he offered us any free drink in the house.

"Another time," Scott told him.

A long single flight of linoleum-covered steps led up to Bartholomew's room. The linoleum might have been bright green upon installation fifty years ago, but no longer. We called from the outside the door, but no one answered. Unlocking the door and entering, we found Bartholomew at the kitchen table staring into a cold cup of coffee.

It took little more than a glance to take in his whole apartment. His living space depressed me. The walls were bare. Everything was clean and spartan. A few carefully mended kitchen chairs sat under a card table. The single bed had an old army blanket, tucked in with military precision, as its only covering. A stack of gay porno magazines peeked from under the side of the bed. Two library books, Greenberg's *The Construction of Homosexuality* and *After the Ball*, by Kirk and Madsen, sat on the nightstand. The only light in the room came from a floor lamp any self-respecting garage sale would reject. An open doorway revealed a spotless john.

He raised two film-covered eyes to us. "I can't," he whispered.

I stayed in the doorway. Scott sat in a creaking chair across from Bartholomew. He took one gnarled old hand from around the coffee cup and held it between his own.

"What's wrong, Bartholomew?" he murmured.

"I'm scared," the old man mumbled. "Scared I'll catch it. Afraid to die."

Patiently Scott explained how you can or can't catch AIDS. He added, "We're all afraid to die, Bartholomew. You can't stop living out of fear. You have to volunteer. To honor Father Sebastian's memory, if nothing else."

The old man stared out the window at the brick wall of the building next door for the longest time. Scott waited, unmoving and silent. His hands around the other man's gave warmth and courage. The old man's pained eyes met Scott's. The deep blue lamps of my lover radiated their warmth.

"I need my coat," Bartholomew said.

We walked him into the clinic. A bright-eyed young man chattering happily took Bartholomew from us and led him away. As he always did when he stopped at the clinic, Scott checked the roster of people with AIDS in area hospitals. He took notes on several new ones and talked to the volunteer to be sure they'd updated his list. Scott visited every person with AIDS in every Chicago hospital, as long as they didn't refuse to see him.

As we left, Bartholomew rushed back to us. "I need to talk to the two of you. I know something about—" He broke off as an attractive young attendant walked up to us.

He smiled at Bartholomew. "I have a blind person with AIDS who needs to be read to this week. We can begin your training

54

later. For now, we have a million envelopes we need help with stuffing." He gave the old man a genuinely warm and caring smile.

Captivated, Bartholomew let himself be led off. "I'll call you tonight," he said over his shoulder as he walked away.

Before we left, we phoned ahead to the Twenty-third District police station, trying to get hold of the Chicago cop Frank had mentioned. He was in. We drove up Halsted to the station. They could have used this place for the run-down precinct station of any urban TV cop show. The cops readily recognized Scott. He signed autographs and chatted happily. The commander came down and greeted him. We got the Cooks tour. When done, he asked if there was anything specific he could do for us. We asked for the man Frank had named, Paul Turner.

With a minimum of curiosity, satisfied by our bland replies and his desire to call everybody he knew to tell about meeting Scott, he led us to a small room on the second floor.

The door stood wide open to reveal a room cluttered with six desks, bookcases, chairs, and barely enough room to walk between all of them. Heaps of paper covered the tops of each desk with only a tiny square open where its occupant could lean an elbow. One man sat in the room, maybe thirty, nice-looking, in a shambling, rugged way. He was the only cop who hadn't clustered eagerly around Scott. The commander introduced him as Detective Paul Turner, the guy we wanted. He told Turner to treat us well. With a final handshake for Scott, he left us. Turner smiled, shook hands, said it was nice to meet both of us. He wore a dull blue tie and a white shirt and nonregulation blue pants; flung over the back of his chair was a herringbone-gray coat that sort of matched his outfit. He wore his shoulder holster and gun. He removed files from two chairs and placed them carefully in order on the floor. I guessed that after we vacated these seats, he would replace the materials exactly as he had found them.

Turner had thick black wiry hair, a quarter inch longer than a brush cut, and at two-thirty in the afternoon he had a five o'clock shadow. He rested his elbows on the table, cupped his chin in his hands, and let his brown eyes gaze at us. If he used that innocent look on me and I was guilty, I'd confess immediately.

I explained our problem from the beginning, leaving out innuendo, sticking to the facts as much as possible. I talked for ten minutes. His attention never wavered.

When I finished he said, "If I hadn't talked to Frank Murphy, I'd toss you both out of here on your asses. I assume you only got this far because nobody in this town would dare question Scott Carpenter or anybody with him. Shitty police procedure, but not hard to understand." At times I had to lean forward to catch his words, spoken in a soft baritone.

"I prefer rules and regulations. You get a dead body. The blues arrive, secure the crime scene. Lab folks show up, take pictures, file reports; detectives ask questions, interview people. Nice, neat, orderly. You two guys are not in the regular order. I think you've found some interesting stuff, but I'm off the case. I'm not supposed to care."

I described Frank's comments on those in charge.

"He shouldn't have told you, no matter how much he trusts you. I like Frank. Maybe it's easier to trust people in the suburbs."

"You don't believe us?" Scott asked.

He smiled briefly at Scott. "Belief isn't my problem at this point. Power and the lack of it are. I'm off the case. I ask why? I'm told to go to work on my other cases. I press the commander. He presses back harder. So I shut up and wonder who's got the clout to push him. Frank tells me documents have disappeared. My sources confirm this. I tried to get official access to the files. No dice. I tried people I know. Nothing. Nobody connected with this case will say word one, not my best contacts. I've been a detective five years. I don't need a road map to see where this is going." He shrugged. "Now you guys show up, outside of regulations and orders. Normally I'd be real interested. But now I've got no questions to ask. It's not my job or my problem. What you've told me adds up to official zip. I could pull in these people, some of whom could squawk real loud. Then I'm in deep shit. For what? A famous baseball player, a concerned schoolteacher, and a dead priest. You guys are out of your league. I'm out of my league. My best advice is, Forget it, boys. If the case has this kind of pull behind it, my guess is people could get very nasty about you poking around."

He twined his hands together, placed them behind his head, and slouched back. No dampness under *his* armpits.

"Do I agree with you? Doesn't matter. Can I do anything for you? Nope, sorry. Would what you say hold up in court? No. Is somebody covering up? Obviously. Should you keep your noses out of it? You bet."

He put his arms down and placed his hands on the table, palms up. "What else can I do for you?"

"What kind of cop are you?" Scott demanded. "Don't you know we're telling the truth?"

The cop smiled. "I think everything you told me was the truth."

"Then what the fuck?" Scott vented his frustration.

The cop never took his eyes away from Scott's face, listening as if he heard your deepest secrets in everything you said. When Scott ran down the cop said, "I'm more frustrated about this than you are."

I believed him.

"I deal in real things. Those I can change. This is one I can't. I'm sorry."

Simple honesty in clear brown eyes.

"If I were on the case, I'd tell you to fuck off as nosy busybodies even if your best friend was the chief of police." He wasn't threatening or being cruel, just expressing his method of working and dealing with amateurs. "Do me one favor?"

I nodded.

"If you find anything out, let me know. If they find you dead, I'll have a start on an investigation."

"If you think we're in danger, why won't you help us?" I asked.

"I don't know if you're in danger. But I don't like the smell of this whole business. Warning you to be careful is all I can do." He shrugged. His shoulders were broad and well muscled.

We got up to leave. Police business over, he said, "My sons would never forgive me if I didn't get Scott Carpenter's autograph. You better sign one for me too." That was refreshing. Usually an adult wouldn't admit it was for him.

He walked us to the door. He took out his wallet, pulled out a card, and gave it to me. "This has my home number, too. I hope you won't need to use it."

We thanked him and left.

We drove back to River's Edge for negotiations with the board of education.

I expected the meeting to last until all hours of the morning. I wanted to confront Clarence the creep, but it would have to wait.

The lawyer for their side took fifteen minutes to deliver the message to the lawyer for our side. The board's basic response to our last offer: Fuck you, go to hell. The mediator, part of the process required in all Illinois school district labor disputes, wrung her hands and requested more meetings. We said bullshit. In fifteen more minutes we acted on the authorization of our members and our vote of Saturday and told them we were ready to strike. I was home by nine. I ranted about asshole administrators for fifteen minutes. Scott's heard the drill several thousand times before. He let me run on, then suggested we confront Clarence.

We didn't call. We drove straight to the rectory. Nobody home. We sat in the car while I fumed. Scott suggested we visit the Manhattan woman friend. Even though it was nearly ten I decided to try it. This wasn't a social call, and maybe a late-evening confrontation with possible exposure of this relationship might shake loose some information.

Half an hour later we strode up the walk. The almost springlike forty-degree temperatures had continued. The woman who met us at the door wore blue jeans and a heavy black sweater. She carried a sleeping baby. We caught a glimpse of Father Clarence in faded jeans and gray sweater lounging on the couch, feet up, gazing at a TV program. He looked in our direction and abruptly sat up straight. We told the woman we wanted to talk to Father Clarence.

"Let them in," he called.

Inside, the woman began to demand to know who we were and what we wanted. Clarence calmed her down. He asked us all to sit. Our voices had waked the baby. Its cries rose quickly to a full bellow. I presumed the woman to be the mother. Probably around twenty-five, she seemed accustomed to the baby, but for whatever reason, her attention torn and her home threatened, her mothering attempts were for nought. The baby squalled louder. Clarence took the kid. Comfortable as he seemed with the child the crying didn't stop. "She's teething," the mother explained, "and your presence doesn't help. It took me an hour to get her quiet." While she directed her anger at me, Scott took the baby from Clarence. The kid stopped crying almost instantly. The man's a wizard.

"How—" The woman reached for her kid, then stopped. The lack of noise eased everybody's tension. Clarence turned off the TV and invited us to sit. He looked like the young executive at home for the evening, in pre-faded designer jeans cut to fit his slender figure. He might work out a day or two a week at a health club. Short hair cut fashionably correct. The apartment had white walls with a few framed posters. All pictured cats in varying stages of cuteness. Burning them would be my first act if it were my place. I can live without cats. The furniture felt comfortable in an overstuffed K-mart way.

We pushed Clarence for answers and information. For fifteen minutes he fended us off.

Finally, frustrated and feeling rotten about doing it, I used the threat of telling about his liaison with the woman and child to get him to talk to us.

At that he rose and stomped about the room, raging at us. I felt guilt, but I wanted information.

He finally sat down, red and puffing. I waited a few minutes and began again. "You're a priest."

His shoulders slumped. He spoke in a dull monotone. "We're married," he said.

"Huh?" I managed.

The woman took his hand and held it gently. "We're in love," she said.

"Who are you?" I said.

"Mrs. Clarence Rogers."

I saw doubt and worry in his look.

"I always wondered what I'd do if this ever happened," he said, more to himself than to us. He looked from Scott to me. "I'm not ashamed of what I've done."

Clarence told us they'd been married five years. She had been a parishioner in his first parish. He didn't feel bound by the outdated precepts of dried-up old men in Rome. "I do a great deal of good as a priest. I won't give it up. I won't give up my sexuality either."

"How does this work?" Scott asked.

"I stay at the rectory only when necessary. I leave after working hours and get back before early Mass. We're very discreet here."

I found the hypocrisy of his lifestyle fascinating.

"Father Sebastian knew all about it. Covered for me numerous times with the chancery. A good guy, but very out of step with the times. When I learned he performed fag masses—"

I interrupted. "Don't say fag."

"You don't like it, complain to the Vatican," he snapped.

"I don't like it, and I'll beat the living shit out of you and mail you to the Vatican if you say it again," Scott said.

Clarence opened his mouth, I thought to make a smart comeback. He stared from one to the other of us. His wife patted his arm and said, "Clare, please."

"What if you're caught?" Scott said.

"They don't burn people at the stake anymore," Clarence said, "as I'm sure you two appreciate. A gay couple or a priest led astray by a woman a few centuries ago might have caused executions. Today, who cares?"

Figuring out we're a gay couple after our comments was not a major trick. We spent fifteen minutes arguing the merits of what my nephew overheard. He continued to insist that Jerry had misunderstood. His wife wanted to know why we wouldn't believe him.

I let it go and switched to asking if he knew anything about Sebastian's private life. "Especially if he had a lover. Any hints at all. Maybe odd phone calls."

"I never paid much attention to the old guy. You get odd phone calls in a rectory all the time," he said.

I thought our presence would be a threat enough to Clarence's lifestyle to get him to open up. Not a chance. After the initial worry he remained as cool and arrogant as if the pope had performed his marriage. I asked if he'd at least let us look around Sebastian's room. He refused, saying the diocese took care of that. He told us nothing helpful.

"Arrogant snot," Scott said in the car.

As we walked to my house from the garage I heard the phone ringing. I hurried in, expecting it to be Bartholomew. Instead, Neil announced that the Faith building had burned to the ground. Worse, they couldn't find Bartholomew. He'd told several people he needed to stop by the Faith offices. He'd borrowed the key from Neil.

We rushed to the city. We found Neil in a cluster of people at the corner of School Street and Clark. He saw us and hurried over. "They found a body," he announced. "I'm afraid. I tried calling his place. No one answered." We hurried to Bartholomew's apartment. We got the bartender to give us the key again.

In the kitchen the few dishes and glasses were carefully arranged in the cupboards. In the refrigerator everything had frozen. Neil explained that Bartholomew had continuous battles with his landlord about fixing things in his apartment. The landlord refused to believe the refrigerator froze everything. Bartholomew took the milk out every night so it would thaw in time for him to put it on his cereal in the morning. The freezer compartment contained five Weight Watchers spaghetti dinners, bought on sale at a Jewel Grocery Store. His windows looked out on garbage cans in an alley.

"I thought accountants made decent money," Scott said.

Neil laughed harshly. "Bartholomew was a victim of history." Neil explained that the man we feared dead in the fire had been dishonorably discharged from the Navy during World War II, caught by an ensign giving blow jobs to half the crew on a submarine. Then he had been unlucky enough in the early fifties to be entrapped by a cop in a Lincoln Park washroom. "A bitter and lonely man, shit on by society, with every right to scream in agony. Mercifully, he never served in prison. With an arrest record and dishonorable discharge, he found it hard to get work. You know, he watched the gay pride parade every year. Each time, I tried to get him to be in it. He always refused, but every year he stood at the corner of Surf and Broadway, clapping and cheering for every group, float, whatever. It became a sort of joke over the years. He stood and clapped as the world passed him by."

"Why was he there tonight?" Scott asked.

"I don't know," Neil said. "It wasn't unusual for him to ask for the keys. He was always forgetting something, his hat, gloves." Neil sighed. "When I got there the whole place was engulfed in flames. The only thing I could get a cop to tell me was that the fire spread awful fast."

"Arson," I said.

5

We returned to the fire scene.

The charred embers and smoke added a murky smell to the neighborhood. The crowd began to drift away. I watched the firefighters sifting through the debris.

I watched Neil and Monica talking to a fire captain. As I turned to make a comment to Scott, I saw Priscilla glance furtively in every direction and then slip around the corner of the LakeView Learning Center, cross the parking lot, and head west on School Street.

I nudged Scott. "Come on." I quickly asked Neil to meet us for dinner the next day, then sped after Priscilla. I explained as we went that I wanted to follow her. I didn't like or trust her. She was too good to be a true as a suspect. Maybe she was up to something tonight. I hoped so. I peered carefully around the building. Walking rapidly, she'd already reached the el tracks. Slipping through shadows we followed her. With only an occasional glance back she hurried six blocks straight west. We paused in the shadow of the Woolworth's doorway on the southwest corner where Lincoln, School, and Marshfield meet. Farther west we traveled to the Northwestern Railroad tracks. Ravenswood Avenue ran north on the east side of the tracks and then south on the west side of the tracks. On the east side it's less than a street but more than an alley, filled with bushes and barbed wire to keep people off the tracks. North we crept past Henderson Avenue, with its grassy parkway down the middle. Then a quick movement under the tracks to the area of town called Roscoe Village, then up the west side of the railroad tracks. Just past Cornelia we lost her. In the shadow cast by the Ravenswood el tracks, crossing high above to soar across the Northwestern tracks, we halted to search the darkness ahead.

We waited several heartbeats, then dashed for the opening she'd passed moments before. I peered around the corner. Nobody in sight, only occasional shadows and silence. Ahead and to the left, numerous semi-trailer trucks lay nestled into loading bays. Mostly we saw the backs of small businesses and one-story factories. On the right, recently repaired barbed wire rose to a height of six feet or more. Feeble light drifted into the darkness in small doses, not enough to cure the urban murk.

Priscilla had either spotted us, and lay hidden, or had entered one of the surrounding doorways. I couldn't see to the far end of the alley. I couldn't tell if it was sealed at the end or even if paths ran along it, providing an escape.

"Stay here," I murmured to Scott and hurried cautiously forward before he could object.

I crept down the left side of the alley, feeling more secure among the crannies and crevices of back yards, garages, and garbage pails than crawling amid the trucks, unhitched trailers, and open bays. From what I could make out in the dim light, most of the delivery bays gaped emptily, stripped of merchandise before giving ideas to nighttime marauders. The distant lights glinted off random truck windows. I'd entered a muffled world of scurrying rats, crumbling concrete, and lurking darkness. Occasionally the sounds of traffic on distant streets drifted into the eerie gloom. The empty windows of the backs of silent factories stared darkly down at me as I eased from one shadow to the next. Training in the Vietnam jungles as a Marine years ago made my senses keenly alert, aware of my surroundings and where possible dangers might lurk.

The slither of tumbling pebbles stopped me. In front or

behind, I couldn't tell. I melted into a deeper shadow next to a crumbling wood fence. The boards of the rickety structure creaked as I crouched against them. I snatched glimpses of the buildings around me, my sight obscured by my crouched position, and listened intently for the recurrence of noise.

Faintly, I heard the whisper of cloth against cloth, definitely behind me. I strained to look over my shoulder, turning only my head, but my shoulder moved and tapped an eighth of an inch of heavy jacket against a loose board. With a whoosh the whole damn fence pitched over. Fortunately the cacophony when it hit the ground made less noise than fireworks in Grant Park on the Fourth of July, but not much less. Anyone listening would think a tank battalion had chosen this moment to rumble up the alley. Still crouched and trying to stop the boards and noise I had unleashed, I bashed my knee against a trash can, which tipped over, spilled its contents, and began rolling away from me.

An instant after silence finally fell, I sensed movement behind me. I whirled in time to see a vast form looming up. Swinging awkwardly from my cramped and crouched position, I managed to land a fist in a midsection. My attacker gave a loud "Oof!" that rang a dim, distant bell. "Scott?" I muttered.

"Motherfucker," he gasped.

He'd fallen toward the light. He sat gasping for breath. I inched over to position myself protectively over him.

"You should have stayed back," I whispered.

"Look, general," he said between pants, "Vietnam was a long time ago. You can give commands to your kids at school, but I'm not waiting out there for you to be beaten to smithereens in here. You don't make my choices."

But for us, the alley remained silent. "I didn't want you in danger," I said.

"Fuck that shit. We're in this together."

"Sorry I hit you," I whispered.

With a final gulp, regular breathing fully restored, he said, "Now what?"

I let my eyes rove around the darkness. "We could try to explore the rest of the alley," I suggested.

He got to his feet and walked boldly to the middle of the alley. "What the hell are you doing?" I demanded.

In a normal voice he said, "Half the universe could have heard us already. If they didn't hear, they're too far away. If they did, they ran."

"Or they could be waiting in ambush," I said.

"Look, Jungle Jim," he said, "I respect all your expertise, but let's cut the shit. We explore the alley without killing each other and then we go home."

"Quietly," I said.

We proceeded, slower than a walk but faster than a patrol through the nighttime jungle. At the end of the alley a twelve-foot chain-link fence blocked our way. To the right, building and fence joined. Between the last building on our left and the fence, a foot-wide path led into further darkness.

Priscilla had either snuck into a building behind us, found a hiding place, or taken a path. I pointed toward the opening. Scott glanced behind us, then toward the deeper darkness of the new opening.

"Let's go back to the street where there's light and see where it comes out at the other end."

A truck started behind us. Headlights snapped on. The cab of an eighteen-wheeler lumbered into the center of the alley and turned toward us.

We both swore.

I heard gears shift. The truck leaped toward us. Heedless of noise, we rushed to the opening. Trash cans flew, along with other unknown obstacles as we kicked them out of our path. The path twisted and turned. With so little light we bumped and stumbled into each other and numerous nameless obstructions. We heard harsh laughter behind us. A final plunge through thick evergreens brought us out onto a sidewalk and busy street.

"Where the hell are we?" I asked.

"I think this is Addison," Scott said.

It was useless to go back, so we trudged over to Clark Street and the car.

We stayed at Scott's Lake Shore Drive penthouse that night. In the morning, after barely four hours' sleep, I sipped coffee in the breakfast nook of the kitchen and watched the early dawn light ease its way over Lake Michigan.

I drove to school for my morning picket duty. The negotiations team members had separate shifts. A few kids showed up to cheer us on. The temperature hovered in the low thirties. Only a few lumps of black-encrusted snow, huddled in the shadows of the school building, reminded us of the storms of December. At eight, two teachers crossed the picket line. Kurt Campbell, our union president, always on duty, remained impassive as we watched them move into the buildings like shamed criminals avoiding the TV news cameras. I boiled with unreasoning fury, which surprised me. Secretly I guess I had told myself all along that this union stuff was peripheral. After all, I had a lover with a fabulous income. Others in the picket line screamed bitter hate at the scabs. For most of my colleagues on the picket line this was their only income, and these people crossing the line threatened their livelihood. It hit me deeply. I had it easy, but I found I cared. All our hard work, and those fools lost their nerve. Kurt had to be impassive. He'd feel responsible about violence, I knew, and he'd see their side, but he didn't try to stop our people from shouting their fury. For his sake I held my tongue. The parents' Strike Support Committee brought us coffee and rolls around nine. The temperature kept us moving and grumbling as we traded places between warm cars parked across the street and the line in front of the school.

At one point late in the morning Kurt thanked me for keeping my cool when the scabs appeared. We sat in my pickup truck and talked over strategy. He'd tried talking to the superintendent of schools informally. No dice. "They're hoping for a below-zero cold wave to break the strike," Kurt said. He sipped coffee from a Styrofoam cup. "Bastards better not underestimate us."

At three my relief showed up. Scott had a photo shoot all day for a fashion magazine. I picked him up on Michigan Avenue in front of the Art Institute.

At five we met Neil for dinner at Genesee Depot. First I asked Neil about Lesbians for Freedom and Dignity, the group Priscilla had mentioned.

He said they were women who'd formed a sort of street gang. Years ago, tired of wimpy men not taking back the streets from rapists and gay bashers, they started patrolling. At first it was three or four of them coming to people's rescue. Over the years they'd grown more and more violent. "Lesbian Radicals from Hell." He snorted. "I don't care what they call themselves, that's what they are, and as humorous as the name sounds, they're dangerous." Police suspected them of bombing church rectories in which pro-life activists held meetings. You heard about the bombing at the chancery a few weeks ago?" Neil asked.

We nodded our heads. A security guard had died in the explosion.

"I have no proof," Neil said, "but I think they were behind it." He'd suspected Priscilla of being one of the guiding lights of the group for some time.

We asked about the break-ins at the *Gay Tribune*. He said there'd been three in the past year, each more destructive than the last. Neil believed Priscilla or Monica or both knew who was doing it, but he had no proof.

We speculated on what information Bartholomew might have had for us. Over dessert I pressed him for more information about Priscilla and the Lesbians for Freedom and Dignity.

"Publicly they disrupt things, but only on a sporadic basis. You've met Priscilla at close to her tamest. You can't imagine a roomful of such women."

He explained that the group might not surface for months at a time. Then, for several weeks, five or six would show up at every community meeting or service, demanding equal repre-

sentation for women and all minority groups, being horrified if
your meeting wasn't wheelchair accessible, insisting that pro-
choice and the ERA be put on the agenda, demanding liaisons
with the feminist community, asking for co-chairpersonships,
co-treasurers, co-secretaries, two for every office, male and
female, on down the line.

"Why not say yes?" I asked after he finished his litany.

I got puzzled looks from both of them. I said, "Put them on
every board and committee. No one could possibly attend all
those meetings and do all that work."

Neil laughed. "They wouldn't do the work even if they did
show up."

"They're nuts," Scott said.

I watched Neil wince in unaccustomed agreement with Scott.
"That, and they're dangerous."

"Surely only to themselves if their keepers give them sharp
objects," I said.

"You're making jokes. These people are committed as only
fanatics can be. But more." He agreed with the police in
believing the Lesbians for Freedom and Dignity were responsible for bombing churches where anti-abortion groups met.
"Nothing's happened in Chicago yet," he said, "but my sources
say they're the ones responsible for three bombings in San
Francisco and one in New York. Lucky for them no one's been
killed."

Somehow I found the whole scenario hard to believe.

"What's kept them in line here?" I asked.

"Think," Neil said. "What keeps most gay and lesbian organizations from maximum effectiveness?"

"Internal bickering," I said.

"Got it in one," Neil said.

We told him about chasing Priscilla and following philander-
ing Clarence.

"Did you know Sebastian was HIV positive?" I asked. In the
confusion of the fire the night before there hadn't been time to
mention it.

Neil looked startled. "I don't believe it."

I told him what we'd learned from the police.

Neil shook his head. "I guess it's true if they found it. He never mentioned having sex with anybody. I've known him for ten years, and he hasn't had any operations where he might have gotten transfusions. Far as I know, he never had any."

"He got it some way. If he knew he had it, he never told anybody, as far as I can tell," I said. "If he could keep that secret, he could obviously keep his mouth shut about how he got it."

After dinner we walked over to the *Gay Tribune* offices. I wanted to see if Monica Verlaine could give us any leads on the Lesbians for Freedom and Dignity. We found her hunched over a computer on the second floor of the office. Not a trace of yesterday's mess remained. They'd covered over the holes in the wall with red poster board. A few staffers sat at the other consoles on both floors, each peering at his or her own screen.

Monica suspected Priscilla was one of the organizers of the women's group but claimed to know little about them.

"Priscilla is widely disliked," she said. "Often that keeps her from getting elected to an office, but she'd be at the center of it. She's perfect for that kind of meeting: energetic, opinionated, unwilling to listen, and out of touch with reality."

"I can see why you're not a member of a nut group, but why aren't you more of a feminist activist?" Scott said.

She gave a pleasant ripple of laughter. She pulled out a cigarette and holder, lit up, took a drag, whirled it in a deft circle around her left shoulder, blew a perfect smoke ring, then said, "I don't have to be. I'm rich. Fuck this powerless movement shit. Take the Lesbian Radicals from Hell—I like Neil's name for them. They have a manifesto of sorts calling for all kinds of absurd kidnappings, bombings, and assassinations. Even if they managed all of it on a large scale, there's no revolution coming. A lot of innocent people could get hurt. They'll fade away and the world will go on very much the same, as if they had never existed. Doing things my way has more positive effect for women than all the bullshit talking they do. By the way, you're wrong to call them a nut group."

"Why's that?" Scott asked.

Monica explained that while she only knew a few of the women involved, she could understand why some of them would be radicalized. She told us about a few of them. One woman, named Stephanie, now grossly overweight and deliberately letting herself look ugly, had started out as one of the most competent emergency-room doctors in Washington, DC. She'd worked long hours without pay with the homeless. Late one night five of the men she'd helped the most had cornered her in a clinic office and raped her repeatedly. Only one of them was ever convicted, and he didn't serve time.

Another woman, named Sally, had grown up in the Catholic ghetto in Belfast. She joined a radical group after her parents had been murdered by a terrorist organization. For a while she tried making a life for herself, working with battered and abused children in the slums of Los Angeles. Her best friend, a man, turned her in to the authorities. "Some of them have good reason to be angry," she said.

I asked about Priscilla, specifically mentioning her actions of the night before and the attack on us with the truck.

Monica didn't know where Priscilla might have been going. She warned us about trying to catch her or interrupt one of the group's meetings. "These people are fanatics," she said. "Generally harmless, but when pushed, who knows? Even I got ugly stares the one time I walked into a meeting, and I was invited." She shrugged. "They've all taken karate, or judo, or some type of self-defense class. Stephenie, the D.C. slum doctor, spent a couple years overseas, training as a terrorist."

"Could Priscilla or members of her group have killed Sebastian?"

Monica puffed thoughtfully on her cigarette for a minute and then said, "No reason. Although a few members of the group do hate the Catholic Church in a generic I-hate-all-religions way." She said the women saw western religions as part of the oppressive patriarchal society. I didn't necessarily disagree with them about that.

We asked her again about the mystery man Sebastian met on Sunday nights. She repeated that she knew nothing.

We walked over to Roscoe's, the bar, with Sebastian's picture. The front room is partly wood-paneled, with a mirrored back wall. One of the charms of Roscoe's is its large front picture window, where you can gaze at the passersby on Halsted Street.

Only a few patrons filled odd corners of the bar on a Tuesday at 8 P.M. The muscular bartender stood maybe five foot six and must have weighed about 160 pounds, giving a fireplug effect. He stared hard at Scott as we ordered our drinks. He brought us two Watney's on draft. Scott held out a twenty to pay for the drinks. The bartender shook his head. "Scott Carpenter doesn't pay in this bar." He paused, then asked almost shyly, "Why are you here? Are you . . ." He let the question dangle.

Scott used to be paranoid about being seen in gay bars. He's gotten much better. Now he simply said, "Yes."

The bartender said, "Oh. Wow. I—oh."

Scott said, "This is my lover, Tom. We need some help."

"Sure. Anything I can do."

We showed him the picture. He nodded immediately. "I recognize the guy in the picture. Can't miss him. We get priests and seminarians in here all the time. He's the only one who wears his priest outfit. You know, that collar Catholic priests wear. He wore it in the bar. He got some odd stares, and a couple of people got real obnoxious. Wanted him to solve their sins and that shit. I had to throw out one guy who got abusive about his childhood in a Catholic school. Wanted your guy in the picture to make it better."

"He ever with anybody?" I asked.

"He was always with some group when I saw him."

"How about just with one person: maybe they looked like lovers?"

He shook his head no. He suggested we try the other

bartenders. They'd be back in about half an hour. Most of them bowled on Roscoe's sponsored bowling team on Tuesday nights. They'd be in after their games for a drink or two. Someone else in the group might know more. We sat on the couch in the back patio room next to the fireplace to wait.

Forty-five minutes later we moved to the front room and saw a happy, smiling, giggling group gathered near the front of the bar. Goosing and shoving each other, they bellied up to the bar in high good spirits. Seems they'd won that night. We strolled over and caught the bartender's eye. He got them quieted enough to listen to us. I thought I saw nods of recognition from several of them on seeing Scott. Gay ex–high-school jocks are pretty much like straight ex–high-school jocks. They read the sports pages, watch games on TV, join the softball league.

The bartender explained what we needed, told them they could trust us. A few doubtful glances, one shrill "Ooh, you two are so cute together!" We showed them the picture. The quietest one, short-haired, with his chin on the shoulder and his arms around a lithe, muscular, effeminate guy, said, "Yeah, I've seen him."

His dark eyes shifted from the picture to us, sad puppy-dog eyes I'd be surprised ever to see smiling happily, set in a likable face. No smile, but pleasant. A few inches shorter than us, but muscular and slim. The face of someone you could talk to.

"I only work part-time Friday and Sunday nights," he explained, moving away from his friend. He tapped the picture. "He comes in every Sunday around midnight. He drinks Chivas on the rocks. I'd say about ninety percent of the time a guy joins him. The priest always arrives here first. He waits for his friend while looking out the picture window."

I asked for a description for the friend.

"Miller Lite, no glass, no tip. Priest always tips a dollar." He paused to think. "Maybe a black-haired guy with his hair all slicked down like from the Fifties. Quiet dresser: button-down shirts and slacks, no jeans. Maybe in his late forties, a slight paunch, but in nice shape. I remember them because it's pretty quiet on Sundays and they're usually here."

"Ever hear them talk?"

He shook his head. "Not to remember."

"A name or anything?"

No luck.

His buddies shook their heads. They'd never seen them at all. According to the bartender who'd seen them, the mystery man hadn't shown up the last two Sundays.

We talked a few minutes. One timid soul asked Scott to autograph a bar napkin. Scott did so. We left them to their celebration. We ordered another round of Watney's and took them to the back room and sat on the couch next to the fireplace. We didn't have much, but it was a start. Several times I tried to start a conversation with Scott. I had my back to the room, and he kept looking over my shoulder. Finally I said "What?" and turned around.

In the same room across from our cozy area, people had gathered around the video machines. One, a pinball game, sat unused. Two men in deep concentration played at the other, a Tetris game. Four guys stood around them, drinks in hand, groaning or cheering at the activity on the screen.

I do not have Nintendo or other video games at my place. I used to play them for hours. Over time Scott brought me several advanced computer programs and games. About four years ago I realized I'd gotten too involved, when the sun rose on me hunched over a video screen and I hadn't been to bed all night. We had a few minor fights and one major blowup about the time I spent playing them. Fortunately, the time I met the sunrise with Nintendo had been during the season while the team was on a road trip. Scott came home to a video-gameless house. He keeps a few at his place for my nephews and nieces to play with when they come over. I control myself and ignore them.

In the bar I couldn't make out clearly the faces of the players.

Scott rested a hand on my shoulder. "Isn't that the cop? What's-his-name, Turner?"

I shifted position. "Which one?"

"At the game. The far one."

I craned my neck. It sure looked like him. Dark-haired, tight blue jeans, a red sweatshirt, white Addidas tennis shoes, eyes glittering, one hand deftly maneuvering the joystick, the other making rapid taps on a control button.

"A cop, here? In a gay bar?"

"Don't be prejudiced," Scott said.

I had visions of undercover cops and entrapment. I moved to join the group, not sure what I wanted to do. Scott followed. The guy working the right-hand control lost with one line left to go over at 90,000 points. The cop passed 140,000 before the game beat him. He laughed and reached behind him to his left to grab his drink from the table. The group drifted away and we moved closer. He held a quarter, but checked his watch as if deciding if he had time for another game.

"You guys go ahead," he said, easing off his chair and looking at us for the first time.

I don't know what I expected, but he smiled and said, "Hi, Tom, Scott. Good to see you." He pointed a thumb at the machine. "You play?"

"What are you doing here?" I demanded.

His smile vanished. He looked from one to the other of us and raised an eyebrow. "Drinking beer and playing video games?" he said.

Scott caught the humor behind the crack and forestalled any comment on my part.

"You on duty?" Scott asked.

"No." Turner smiled. Matter-of-factly he said, "All three of us are gay."

"Oh," I said. I'd never met a gay cop before, never pictured one as thirty, good-looking, and athletic.

We sat together for a while, sharing notes on the various degrees of closetedness forced on us by our disparate jobs.

Turner seemed quite comfortable. He pointed to Scott. "You don't announce it on the pitcher's mound." He turned to me. "You don't announce it in front of your classroom, and I don't announce it to the squad room. Our friends know. My family knows, and they cope in one way or another, just like us."

We told Turner what we'd found out. He said he'd be interested in talking to the mystery man, if we could find him, but he didn't think it would do any good.

"Look, you guys," he said. "You're not going to get anywhere. First of all, you've got to prove it's a murder, figure out how somebody did it and why, all without making it obvious to anyone you're investigating."

I interrupted. "Maybe they used a drug or poison."

"Possible. Prove it."

I couldn't, so I shut up.

"You've talked to people, just like I did. The guy was a goddamn saint. Nobody had a reason to kill him." He took a slug of beer. "Yeah, it's suspicious that the chancery and half the cops in the city are covering up. Maybe the church doesn't want people to know some of their priests are HIV positive."

On occasion I'd read about priests dying of AIDS, nothing widely discussed, often with the distinct impression the church was doing its best to pretend it hadn't happened. I asked him if he'd heard about Lesbians for Freedom and Dignity.

"The group they call Lesbian Radicals from Hell?"

Obviously more people than just Neil knew the pejorative nickname for the group.

Turner explained that the police didn't buy into conspiracy theories as much as they did in the days of the infamous Chicago Red Squads. Back in the late sixties and early seventies the cops had spied on peace groups and other activists. Suits had been filed, a stink raised, and finally the cops had lost in court. "I take them seriously a little more than some because I've heard from guys who've covered events they've tried to screw up."

He proceeded to describe the fanatical nature of the women

who wore the green and white Lesbian Radical from Hell buttons and T-shirts. On occasion they drove the cops nuts. Nowadays police received training in being restrained, but these women never let up. So far the women had stopped short of physical violence but had given themselves up for arrest. A police record was claimed as a badge of honor, those women without one being something less than true radicals.

He checked his watch again and excused himself. "It's after nine. I've got to pick my kid up from a seminar he's been to at the Latin School."

After he retrieved his coat from the top of the video machine he came back over to us. "Drop it, you guys. Seriously. It could only get dangerous and people could be hurt." He leaned closer. "No, I haven't given up my investigation. I'm too good a cop to let them stop me, but I've got to be careful. You guys can only get hurt." He shook hands with us and left.

At Scott's the answering machine blinked red off and on. My brother Glen's voice told me to call him no matter what time we got in. It was just after midnight and I thought of not doing it, but I'd never had that kind of message from him before. I punched in his number. Glen snatched up the phone before the end of the first ring.

"Jerry's missing!" he announced.

◄ 6 ◄

The boy had been expected home from a basketball game at six. By seven his parents were angry he hadn't called. By nine they'd called all of Jerry's friends and the school. By eleven they were frantic. Now, after midnight, they were scared. They'd called the police, who promised they'd do what they could after he'd been gone twenty-four hours. His coach and teachers said he had an uneventful day at school, followed by a normal basketball game: scored ten points, made a couple of great steals. No failing grades, no fights with another kid. Jerry'd been seen walking home by himself on the same path he'd used since third grade. It was a three-quarter-mile stretch, well lit, with no dark spots for lurking attackers. All these years he'd traversed it uneventfully. I remembered years ago he insisted he wasn't a baby and could walk it by himself. His concerned parents had shadowed him for a week. They'd discovered a network of parents who watched the same streets and corners, joined the group, and worried less.

I felt guilty about not telling Glen about Father Clarence's threats. After I got off the phone I called the rectory. I got the damn answering machine. I hoped their parishioners would revolt against the lazy shits and their mechanical approach to crisis.

Scott suggested calling Father Clarence in Manhattan. Directory assistance found the number listed under the last name and first initial. I dialed and got an answering machine. We debated going in person and decided first thing in the morning would be just as good.

I paced the floor for an hour. Scott does what he does when he's upset. Late as it was, he headed for the gym down on the second floor of the penthouse. After a while I joined him. Together we punished the machines for half an hour.

I wound up curled in a chair in the living room, falling asleep around five. At six he woke me. The alarm had gone off. I had to get to school. He came with me. He'd go straight to Glen's house. I'd join them after picketing, and together we'd confront Clarence.

First thing, I got hold of Kurt and explained the situation to him. He told me to forget the union, asked me if he could do anything. I told him I'd let him know. From Glen's I phoned Frank Murphy, the River's Edge cop. He had no news, promised to push as hard as he could to find Jerry. While Glen and Jeanette went to school to question or requestion Jerry's friends, classmates, and teachers, we drove to the rectory. We didn't see the red Corvette but, being unsure of his habits, stopped anyway, on the off chance Clarence had come in from Manhattan without it.

Two tiny old women in cobbler aprons met us at the door. The one with blue-rinsed hair clutched a mop in her right hand. The one with tightly curled gray hair carried a can of Lysol in her left hand. With some reluctance they agreed to let us in to see the secretary. We found her pacing a luxurious first-floor office: deep, soft, wine-red rugs, leather-backed and cushioned chairs, polished wood, six-foot-by-three-foot desk. Gold-embossed spines of books looked at us from floor-to-ceiling bookcases.

Constance Madison, the secretary, shooed the other two women out and demanded to know what we wanted. As I explained about Jerry being missing and the questions surrounding Father Sebastian's death, she twirled her wedding ring with long thin fingers. She was gray-haired, with oversized glasses on a sharp pinched nose. Her plain black dress draped the thin figure of a woman in her late fifties. When we asked to speak to Clarence, she told us to get out and slammed the front door after us.

As I started my truck, the little old woman with the blue rinsed hair peeked around the back of the house. She poked her nose furtively in several directions, then gestured frantically for us to come over.

We leaped out of the truck. Our feet left indentations in the recently thawed earth on the side of the house, perhaps a garden in summer. The woman clutched a faded red babushka around her head but wore no coat. She spoke in a crackly old voice. "Quick, follow me." She led us back into the house. We stopped in a cluttered entryway. Winter coats hung on racks to our left, a row of boots under them. A window in the door let in the winter light. "Harriet," she whispered.

From the door opposite emerged the other little old woman. They faced us with their arms entwined. We towered at least a foot above them.

"We must be quick, Mildred," Harriet said.

Mildred gulped. "Yes, if Constance knew we'd talked to you, she'd yell at us again."

They might have been twins. Mildred had removed her babushka and clutched it in one hand, occasionally dabbing at the side of her face with it.

Harriet patted her tightly curled gray hair and said, "We listened at the door."

"We usually don't," Mildred said. "It's rude and none of our business, but we heard you talking about Father Sebastian's death. We couldn't let you leave. He was so wonderful, and Harriet's a baseball fan so she recognized Mr. Carpenter." She tittered. "You're both such good-looking young men."

Harriet said, "We want to help. I can tell you Father Clarence isn't here. We don't know where he is, do we?" They looked at each other for confirmation.

Mildred said, "Such a handsome and well-spoken young man." She sniffed. "At least he doesn't treat us cruelly like that"—she hesitated, then finished—"that beast, Constance."

Harriet said, "But no one was nicer than Father Sebastian." They chirped together about his kindness for several moments.

I controlled my growing impatience. "You wanted to see us," I said.

Eventually Mildred told the story. Ever since Father Sebastian died the rectory had been in chaos. The temporary assistant wanted to change too much. They'd worked there for over twenty-five years together. They would never repeat gossip, but they knew secrets.

They knew all about Clarence's nocturnal comings and goings. "Priests are supposed to stay in the rectory," Mildred said. "Sometimes he's out every night of the week."

Harriet arched an eyebrow, "Sometimes for weeks in a row."

"How do you know all this?" I asked.

"We live over there." Mildred pointed out the window and across the street. I saw a little rectangular box of dirty red bricks, two front windows, and a screenless front door. A 1951 Packard in mint condition sat in the driveway. "I'm awake very late every night," she said.

"And I wake up early every day," Harriet said. "I'm up at five every morning. I see him sneaking in."

"Maybe he's got an apartment somewhere," I said.

They gave me pitying looks. "He lies about where he goes," Mildred said. "We've heard him tell people he slept in the rectory. Nobody knows he leaves except us."

"Father Sebastian knew," Harriet amended.

"Yes, such a saint." Mildred sighed. "He covered up for Father Clarence. Young people make so many foolish mistakes, and Father Sebastian helped him so much."

"But Father Sebastian knew?" I asked.

Mildred glanced at the door, leaned toward us, and whispered, "Yes, but he didn't approve."

"They had angry words," Harriet said. "Father Sebastian didn't approve of his caterwauling all night."

I asked them when this was.

"About two years ago, soon after Father Clarence arrived," Mildred said. "Father Clarence had a lot of modern ideas. He'd only talk to people during business hours. He made Father Sebastian get the answering machine. Father Clarence wanted to run the parish like a corporation."

"No heart or soul," Harriet said. "No people dropping by just to visit. Everybody had to have appointments."

"Did the priests quarrel often?" I asked.

"No. Father Sebastian wasn't a fighter. I think he lost his temper that one time in a moment of weakness. He had the flu that week. I remember because I had to make a trip to the old neighborhood in Chicago to get the proper ingredients for an old family cure," Mildred said.

Harriet smiled. "It always works."

Mildred continued. "They yelled while he was sick, but I heard Father Sebastian apologize a week later."

Harriet nodded agreement. "Most of the time they got along very well."

The nodded their heads in unison at the end of each sentence as a kind of visual punctuation.

Worry about Constance seemingly forgotten, I let them run on about life at the rectory. Most of it was of little use. They did tell us that chancery officials had been crawling all over the rectory for two weeks. For the first few days after Sebastian's death, Clarence had stayed in almost every night.

I asked if we could see Father Sebastian and Father Clarence's rooms.

They exchanged nervous looks, tittered behind their hands, and nodded simultaneous agreement. They took us through the door, with rapid peeks in all directions including behind us, then into the kitchen, down the main hall, and a quick left up a sweeping grand staircase. From the office area on the main floor came the soft *thwack-thwack* of paper exiting a copying machine.

Upstairs they led us to the left past closed doors, two on the left, three on the right. Harriet fumbled rapidly through a set of keys and unlocked the last door on the right. "Father Clarence's room," she announced as she led us in. After we entered, Mildred stood guard at the door. Father Clarence obviously didn't believe that cleanliness was next to godliness. Several pairs of sweat socks and a jock strap formed a small mound in front of the closet. A blue dress shirt had strayed several feet from this pile. A heap of bed linen fought with numerous pillows for the right to center stage on the bed.

The dresser had a framed portrait of a family. A young Father Clarence smiled at us along with an older male and female and several teenagers, at a guess his parents, brother, and sister. From the dresser top I took a small heap of mail, all ads and bills.

Suddenly Mildred hissed, "Someone's coming!" She whisked the door shut and joined us.

We held our breaths in the middle of the floor, but the footsteps never approached our door. They faded, returned, moved deliberately down the stairs.

We breathed again and resumed searching. Scott checked the closet. I looked rapidly through the materials in the dresser. In the top drawer rested the largest, most jumbled collection of bikini briefs I'd ever seen. In my quick look through it seemed as if Clarence hadn't duplicated one color or pattern. Nothing incriminating or even remotely interesting jumped out of any of the drawers.

I finished the dresser and began hunting through the bathroom. Toothbrush, aspirin, vitamin C, Centrum multivitamin, two different brands of suntan oil, a jumble of fingernail and toenail clippers. All in all, no hidden passage, stash of illegal drugs, or secret note admitting to murder or kidnapping.

Again at the door, the women repeated their searching looks, concluding with nods to each other, and off we tiptoed down the way we came, past the stairs and into the first door on our left.

"Sebastian's old room," Harriet whispered.

The older priest merited a suite. The first room had dark gold wall-to-wall carpeting interrupted only by a rectangle of tiles in front of a fireplace in which sat a neat pile of logs on a grate, but no ash underneath—lack of use or incredible tidiness. Light gold drapes matched the carpet. Brown leather love seats faced each other in front of sliding glass doors that led to a small balcony. We'd taken several steps toward the bedroom when Mildred sounded her warning. This time as we huddled together the door opened. Constance Madison stared angrily. In obedience to her command we marched downstairs. The three of them stayed behind. Downstairs in the kitchen we heard loud shouts from upstairs, the voices making remarkably loud and distinctly unChristian comments back and forth.

While we paused to listen, Father Clarence walked in. He stopped abruptly when he saw us. "What the hell are you two doing here?"

"Jerry's been kidnapped," I said.

"Your nephew? That's outrageous." His surprise and shock didn't seem fake. "You think I had something to do with it because of what he said."

"Cut the crap," I said. "He didn't lie. He heard something. You're the direct link. We want answers, explanations, and alibis, if you have them."

We all heard renewed raised voices from upstairs at the same time. We explained, then followed as he hurried through the house and up the stairs. We stood in the doorway while he straightened out the mess. Turned out Mildred and Harriet's last name was Weber. After he'd established a truce he told them we needed to talk.

The Weber sisters managed to trip and chirp over every object in an unhurried trek to the hall. I imagined Constance would keep them from listening at the door.

We sat opposite him on the leather couches. From there I

could see out the sliding-glass double door beyond the balcony to a cloudless day and a few remaining patches of snow on the ground.

He couldn't have done the kidnapping, he said. He'd been with his wife since noon yesterday. It was his day off, and they'd driven to Rockford for shopping. They tried to socialize in distant cities and suburbs to avoid accidental encounters with parishioners.

"You could have organized it," Scott said.

"With an alibi I couldn't use except to people like you?" he said. "That makes no sense."

"Somebody did it, and you had the best reason," I said. "We want to know whom you were talking to the other day after Mass and what was said. If you don't tell us, we blow the whistle on your sex life. A little nooky is one thing. A full-blown marriage, and a kid is another."

He got up and paced the room, touching the fixtures, adjusting his Roman collar. He wound up at the sliding doors, tapping his knuckles against the pane.

"I thought I could stop by becoming a priest." He turned to us. "Girls have thrown themselves at me since before puberty. I learned about sex fast, but I knew it was wrong." He held out his hands to us, pleading. "I honestly believed as a kid that when I had intercourse outside of marriage, it was a mortal sin. It got so I'd have sex with a girl, then run to confession. I couldn't stop either habit. I liked being popular, and the girls turned me on. I never told them about my horrible guilt feelings, but I couldn't stop myself."

He returned to the couch, sat back, and closed his eyes.

"You're the first ones I've told this to outside of confession." He sighed deeply, reopened his eyes, and resumed his story. "At each confession I'd tell only the individual sin. I'd switch from priest to priest at different parishes. Even with the seal of confession I was petrified. I was afraid the priests would recognize my voice. I think one guy did." He winced. "I prayed and repented, but the next week I'd do it again. I thought as a priest it'd get easier. In the seminary they kept us away from most outside influence, so I didn't have much of a problem. I didn't have any trouble fending off the fags."

"Gay people," Scott reminded him.

"Oh, yeah, right," Clarence said. "Anyway, being away from women helped. I've never been into jacking off. I'd always had an outlet. I might have beat off five times in my life." He shrugged. "Anyway, I got out of the seminary, and it started all over. My first day of office hours in my first rectory, I met my future wife."

He gave us chapter and verse of his fairly ordinary double standard. He even told us about cheating on his girlfriend with a number of flings each place he'd been stationed.

Once she got pregnant, he agreed to marry her. They moved down to the Manhattan area after he got assigned to St. Joseph's.

He talked for nearly fifteen minutes, maybe glad for a chance to finally tell somebody a little ordinary truth. I held myself in check while he unburdened himself. Oddly enough, while I thought he was a sexual idiot, I felt a little sorry for him, torn as he was between pleasure and punishment.

"Tell us about the fight with Sebastian," I said.

"Who told you about that?" he asked.

I glared. "We ask the questions. You give the answers."

His right fist clenched a moment, and he threw a string of unpriestly epithets at us, but he didn't get up to leave or try to throw us out.

After he ran down, I said, "I want your entire relationship with Sebastian, honestly detailed."

After a few more spurts of wounded pride, he told us. He and the old priest had existed in tenuous truce. For two years, they had agreed not to tell the chancery about each other. Sebastian had questioned Clarence the morning after he stayed out all night from the rectory for the first time. Clarence knew he needed a cover, so instead of denying his sexual activity, he suggested a deal.

Sebastian's continued involvement in Faith, after being specifically ordered not to, could have caused him some major problems. Clarence agreed not to report him and to cover for him if necessary. In return Sebastian would maintain silence about Clarence's married life.

Clarence explained about wanting to stay a priest, emphasizing the good he could do for people. He wanted both worlds and would fight to keep them.

"Sebastian didn't raise much objection. Maybe he really was the saint everybody says he was. I think he felt sorry for me. I'm probably the first actively heterosexual priest he ever met. How could he talk? If I had told on him, he'd be in just as deep shit as me."

"What about what Jerry overheard?" I said.

This was a pure accident according to Clarence. He'd never have threatened Jerry if he hadn't been so startled.

It seems an official high in the diocesan hierarchy had come to give him a friendly warning. Word in the chancery was that they had to cover up the real cause of Sebastian's death, but that an internal investigation of the priests in the parish, already secretly under way for some months, would be expanded. Rumors of sexual irregularities in, at, or connected with St. Joseph's rectory had reached too far up in the hierarchy to be ignored. Clarence didn't know why there needed to be a cover-up of the cause of death. He hadn't been terribly interested because of the threat the sexual investigation posed to his own safety.

On that day Clarence had panicked at the news. He told the official everything he knew about Sebastian's gay life and then confessed to sexual indiscretion. The chancery official was an old friend of Sebastian's and someone Clarence trusted from his seminary days. The friend promised to delay any investigation as much as possible, giving Clarence time to decide if he wanted to stay a priest, get a divorce, or find some unknown third solution. The friend had left. Clarence, relieved but still badly shaken, heard the noise and stumbled on Jerry. Fury at another part of his life out of his control caused him to lose his temper at the boy.

I asked for the name of the chancery official; we'd have to talk to him. Reluctantly, under pressure, he told us it was Auxiliary Bishop John Smith. We also got access to Father Sebastian's room.

As we began our search Clarence said, "I don't think it'll do you any good. A couple of old guys, priests from the diocese, came by the day after the funeral and took out maybe a suitcase full of stuff." Clarence didn't know of any family Sebastian might have. He thought he spent most holidays with an old friend or two from his seminary days. "I got the impression," Clarence said, "that the ones who cleaned the room were old friends of his. They took only the immediately personal stuff." He only knew that the priests came from the chancery and that it was a normal occurrence when a priest died with no family for someone from the central office to take care of things.

I told him I wanted him to call ahead to his buddy in the chancery to set up a meeting and to smooth our way. With some reluctance, he did so as we listened. Then we searched Sebastian's room and found absolutely nothing at all connected with murder. The combination of chancery office and the probable cleaning by the Weber sisters had made it totally antiseptic.

As we prepared to go I asked if he knew of any possible love interest in Sebastian's life.

He shook his head. "The guy believed in his chastity vow. He refused to judge others, but held himself to a rigid moral code. I can see him becoming very close to somebody but not consummating the union, if that's what gays call it."

"Some of us call it that," Scott said. We left him standing in the middle of the room. A quick stop at Glen's found the parents sitting worriedly on the couch without a lead to pursue. I explained how the disappearance might have been connected to Sebastian's death. They seemed to prefer that explanation to assuming some child molester had got hold of him. Glen had no problem with my keeping Jerry's secret. He said, "What would we have done differently if we knew? The kid's been making his way home for years by himself." We promised to do whatever we could to help find him.

In the city at Scott's penthouse we found a message on his machine from his parents. His relationship with them is tricky. His status as the winningest pitcher in baseball for the past ten years and the highest paid player in the game is a source of intense pride for them. As he won more games, their standing in Waskalosa, Alabama, soared from that of backwoods dirt-poor farmers to a reflected national celebrity. Plus Scott gave them a new home and enough money to enjoy a comfortable retirement. After he came out to them, their back-country born-again Baptist roots kept them from seeing or talking to him for months. The rest of his family, especially Scott's favorite sister, had worked on them to change. Despite their initial rejection and hurt, he'd continued to send them a monthly check, and they'd continued to cash it. Starting the Paris negotiations to end the Vietnam War was easy compared to what he went through before their visit. They insisted on staying in a hotel. Scott's got enough room at his place to house the entire population of Waskalosa.

I'd told him if my being out of the way would help, I would understand. That got me an icy no. He's never mentioned it, but I think the positive reception we get from my parents, brothers, sister, nephews, and nieces adds to his sense of frustration when dealing with his parents.

His parents' message said that because of all the recent airline accidents, perhaps they should wait a few weeks, then take the train. Scott called them immediately. How he can remain so calm while talking to them is beyond me. His deep voice rumbled assurances to Waskalosa for several minutes before he hung up.

He came and sat next to me on the couch overlooking the view of the Loop.

"We could go to Alabama," I suggested.

"Nope. Here," he said. "My territory. My lover. They've had time to get used to the idea of us. I'd also like them to meet your family."

"If you can get yours to agree, I'm sure my mom and dad would cooperate." He nodded thoughtfully. We changed and went down to his second-floor gym. We used the machines and weights for an hour.

At four we hurried to meet Monica Verlaine and Neil at the *Gay Tribune* office. Neil appeared in a well-tailored navy blue business suit. Monica wore a rust-colored velvet pant suit with a wide back belt and a scarf that draped from shoulder to waist, wide at the top, narrow at the bottom, colored a red, orange, yellow, and rust paisley.

I brought them up to date about Jerry, Clarence, and the chancery. I mentioned the possibility of the Lesbians for Freedom and Dignity kidnapping Jerry.

"Priscilla was her usual self today at work," Monica said. "She fought with two advertisers, screamed at a receptionist, and balanced the books." She gave a grim smile. "I don't know enough about that group to know if they'd do kidnapping or not, or in this case why. I can't see a benefit for them."

Neil said, "They don't work by reason. Who knows why? I think the real obstacle is their inability to make decisions and act on them. Priscilla can organize books, figures, an office, but she can't organize people. A lot of people resent her. It was a mistake to elect her head of Faith. Her group is too bumbling to get to the suburbs, take the kid, and hide him successfully."

Scott said, "According to what you and the cop said, they have done some successful violence."

"Mickey Mouse shit," Neil said, dismissing their past activities.

I said, "They could have hurt Jerry."

"Not deliberately," Monica said.

"Accidentally or any other way, they better not," Scott said.

We left the newspaper and drove to the cathedral rectory, where we had our appointment with Clarence's mystery man from Sunday. Many of the priests who worked in the chancery lived at the cathedral rectory only a few blocks away. We parked on State Street and walked up the wide stone steps to the front door.

A young priest opened the door and ushered us into a first-floor hall that had a black-and-white checkered tile floor, down the center of which ran a mahogany-colored rug. We went up a formal staircase to the second floor, where the decor changed. This was all quiet elegance in a gay Gothic sort of way. Fifties religious articles filled small tables at regular intervals down the hall. We stepped on plush deep-blue carpeting. Various cardinals, bishops, and archbishops from Chicago's past peered across at one another from portraits along the length of the hall that the young man led us down. We passed a room painted outrageously green.

The priest walked with his hands concealed in the long sleeves of his cassock. He had a fresh round face, all glowing red cheeks and frowning decorum. He led us to the office of the Rev. John Smith, one of Chicago's numerous low-level auxiliary bishops. Just outside the door, our guide's frozen look broke long enough for him to request an autograph from Scott, who signed the back of a holy card the priest produced from the depths of his cassock. "Thank you," he whispered gratefully, then leaned closer. "I'm a big fan of yours, Mr. Carpenter." He melted away down the hall.

I gave a knock. A soft murmur bade us enter.

We walked onto a blue carpet thicker and even deeper in color than in the corridor. White oak paneling covered three of the walls. The room might have been a sitting or drawing room in a nineteenth-century mansion. A set of hard-cushioned chairs and a settee were placed around a window whose heavy three-quarters-closed navy blue drapes shut out the blur of the cathedral next door. Paintings of religious shrines, properly lighted and hanging at regular distances from one another, adorned the walls. I recognized Fatima and Lourdes. One or two other chairs, best described as indoor graveyard furniture, were scattered about the room. Brass lamps on delicate side tables provided light from either side of the settee. A man in an impeccably tailored black suit and Roman collar rose to greet us from the seat at the window.

Father John Smith had a full head of black hair, a clean-shaven face, the aforementioned perfect suit, and a Roman collar, along with the most highly polished black shoes I'd ever seen, including my time in the Marines. I guessed him to be in his mid-fifties.

"Welcome," he murmured. He offered and I shook a soft, damp, fish-shaped hand. He led us to the chairs opposite the settee. As we sat, he offered us tea. We declined. High tea at the cathedral rectory. Next they'd invite us to Solemn High Vespers.

He began with consolation. "You have my deepest sympathy in the matter of your missing nephew. I pray for his immediate safe return." He proceeded to chat about the baseball season and about teaching school and gave us minor tidbits of idle gossip about the new archbishop's getting used to his position. Cardinal Bernardin had been elevated to Prefect of the Congregation of Religious in Rome. The new man had arrived three months before.

Tiring of his smooth chatter, I broke in. "We're here about Father Sebastian's death."

My change of topic occurred without a murmur or hint of discomfort on his part. I explained our concern, and our knowledge of a cover-up on the part of church officials, and demanded information.

He smiled, took a bite of cookie, a sip of tea, replaced saucer and cup on the tray, and wiped each finger individually with a monogrammed cloth napkin, which he then proceeded to fold neatly and place next to his teacup. If he touches one more thing on that tray I thought, there'll be another death in the clergy.

But he didn't. He crossed one leg over the other, steepled his hands, and placed the tips under his chin. "The situation at St.

Joseph's Church is most unfortunate. We need to find the most diplomatic way to resolve all the issues involved."

"You've got a possible murder, a married priest with a baby, and a possible kidnapping by one of your priests."

"You have no proof for your first and last assumptions," he said. Smith was the kind of guy who, when he was a kid, loudly dealt out insults begging for fights so he could run and tell teacher when someone finally got mad enough to beat the shit out of him. In college, his kind organized study groups to show off how much more he knew than anybody else the night before the test. He would brag about an A paper, hoping you got an F. He was a nerd with a chip on his shoulder.

"Why is there a cover-up?" Scott asked. "And how can you get the police to go along with it?"

The entire output of the spring run of Vermont maple syrup was as nothing compared to the sugared tone the priest now adopted.

"We don't expect outsiders to understand the workings of Holy Mother Church," he said. "History has proven we know what is best. You speak of matters you can't possibly fathom. We need to leave these complicated matters in the hands of those of us who are used to dealing with such issues."

"You mean lots of priests die every year whose deaths you have to cover up?" Scott asked.

"I refer, of course, to the level of complexity rather than specific issues," Father Smith replied.

"What happens to Father Clarence?" I asked.

"After a decent interval he'll be transferred to a quiet parish."

"And the woman?" I asked.

"We have ways of dealing with such issues that I'm not at liberty to discuss. Suffice it to say that most of the women in earlier cases have found it advantageous not to make a public scandal." He harrumphed. "I'm sure you're not naïve enough to think that Father Clarence is unique."

"I thought the kid might be a little unusual," I said.

"A trifle," he conceded, "but well within the ability of this diocese to handle."

"Like you cover up for priests who molest kids," Scott said.

"You raise an unfortunate issue. Yes, we have priests with faults. Some are alcoholics, a few are thieves. Jealousy, ambition: we are not exempt from human vices. You judge us harshly?"

"You bet your ass I do. You're in the do-good business. You set yourselves up as better," Scott said.

"Some people might direct the same kind of comment towards you as a baseball player and gay man. I make no judgment. In the church we try our best. Some fail. Most are good priests doing excellent work in thousands of quiet ways for good and decent people."

I said, "Father Clarence told us about the cover-up."

Another sugary smile appeared. "Please, gentlemen. He's a frightened man with his world crumbling around him. It's unfortunate your nephew misunderstood some garbled words."

I began a protest, but he held up a hand to forestall me.

"Spare me. You're intelligent men. You've told some of your suspicions to the police." It was a statement, not a question, but I nodded anyway. "Well, they haven't been here," he continued. "If they choose to give no credence to a twelve-year-old, who am I to insist to the contrary?"

"You pompous son of a bitch," I said.

He chuckled. "That's been said to me since first grade. I find it a natural ability that is essential in my job as diocesan trouble shooter." He paused, rubbed a hand thoughtfully along his jaw, then resumed. "I have a bit of advice for you gentlemen. Don't you think it better for your reputations, and because of the nature of your relationship, to avoid the possible publicity and inherent dangers of this kind of meddling?"

I smiled and Scott laughed out loud. My lover said, "I guess you think you're making a threat. We aren't impressed. The truth's coming out with or without your help."

In the middle of the silent elegance of the room, Smith calmly

94

raised an eyebrow. "Is there anything else I can do for you gentlemen?"

On the street I said to Scott, "I feel like I've just been raped by the entire Chicago Bears football team at high noon in the center of Daley Plaza, and no one's going to do anything about it."

"You know," Scott said. "Change that black suit and collar to a button-down shirt and gray sweater, and he could be the guy the bartender at Roscoe's described who met Sebastian on Sundays."

Scott was right. I thought of going back and asking, but assumed that the most we'd get was another suave denial.

We had several hours to kill before our next appointment. I wanted to try following Priscilla again. Monica and Neil had told us she'd be at a Neighborhood Crime Watch meeting at Halsted and Aldine until ten.

We dined at My Brother's Place in its usual quiet elegance. We don't get there often enough.

We hit the streets around nine-thirty to be buffeted by a rising wind off the lake. On the car radio we heard that the National Weather Service had issued a winter storm watch for the metropolitan area. If the temperature plummeted close enough to freezing, we could be in for some nasty weather. At the moment, fifty-degree temperatures held.

7

Even though we'd given ourselves extra time, we almost missed Priscilla. We couldn't find a parking space anywhere near the Beat Representative Office of the Twenty-third District. In Chicago each police district has a Beat Representative program. It's sort of like a community relations office with overtones of ombudsperson thrown in. As opposed to the bad old days of Chicago police riots, nowadays the department is more conscious of the necessity of positive dealings with the non-crime-committing sector of the public.

We wound up having to park south of Belmont and had to hurry back through the gathering wind.

Our plan of attack was simple: Follow Priscilla. All the church leads seemed such dead ends I wanted to chance chasing her despite any risks, and as small as the possibility was that it would lead to the solution of Father Sebastian's death. Since last night's fiasco, we wanted to be sure she hadn't taken precautions against our following her. Certainly she'd be cautious, might even have someone follow her to be extra safe. If a shadow protector existed tonight, even if we lost Priscilla, we could follow that other person to a hiding or meeting place.

Through the plate-glass windows we saw the group members standing in small clusters, pulling on winter garments. We hid in the shadows up Aldyne. We'd approached down the cross alley from Melrose and met no one. Facing due east, we felt the force of a rising wind almost directly in our faces.

Priscilla stood at the door in what looked like amiable conversation with a uniformed officer. Moments later she finished pulling on her gloves and strode out the door. She turned north on Halsted. We waited.

A minute passed. Scott whispered, "We'll lose her if there's no protector and we don't follow soon."

Fortunately, none of the others had walked north. A few waited at the bus stop across the street. Others had scattered in different directions. I began to move forward but caught myself at the last second. A well-muffled figure stepped from the shadows on the other side of Halsted. The layers of heavy winter clothes prevented identifying it as male or female. I saw a short person in jeans with glasses under a furry hat who turned north also.

"Is that the one?" Scott asked.

I shrugged. We were just starting out, and already our plan had serious flaws. "We've got to try it," I said.

Following turned out to be surprisingly easy. The figure peered carefully from side to side and forward into every shadow but, fully confident in the role of protector, never looked back. After a few moments of following, I felt much better. We caught occasional glimpses of Priscilla a block and a half ahead. Up Halsted we went, past Addison, with a darkened Cubs park a few blocks west, glanced in the windows of the Twenty-third District police station, beyond a few gay bars and the bus turnaround to where Halsted ends at Grace. There our little parade continued up Broadway all the way to Irving Park.

With no hesitation we followed the westward turn down Irving Park. With the wind now at our backs, walking became far more comfortable. At any time Priscilla could suddenly have taken a car, hailed a taxi, or been joined by a friend, any of a thousand possibilities. Fortunately, she walked on. I was determined to keep following until we got whatever information we could get. I knew we didn't have any factual evidence, but Priscilla was right up there with Father Clarence at the top of my kidnappers list.

When we got to Graceland Cemetery, following became more difficult. The south side of Irving Park Road has a chain link fence and no possibility of concealment. The north side of the street has a brick wall with extremely limited hiding places. We found one spot where the wall jutted out and waited. We saw the protector cross Clark Street. We hurried forward, still staying on the opposite side of the street. The figure passed the Burger King and post office and kept going.

On the right up ahead loomed the mass of Lake View High School. Across from it on the block between Greenview and Ashland stood a structure that surpassed the high school in immensity.

At the corner of Greenview and Irving Park, the protector gave several last searching glances around. From our hiding place a half block away, we could see clearly. On the last few blocks he or she had been much less careful. After a last look back, the person scuttled down Greenview. We hurried forward.

The structure was a huge old church-school complex, all interconnected. It took up more than two thirds of the block. We were in time to see the protector slip through the hedge surrounding the complex.

For a moment an indoor light silhouetted him or her in a recessed opening in the building.

Carefully, in case they'd set up observers, we explored the outer perimeter of the structure. It looked to be a church school from the old days when religion was the center of community life. I'd been to enough meetings of gay activist committees in such structures to make a fair guess at the interior from the placement of the windows. The front half consisted of church on the top floor, with offices on the ground floor under it. The back half, several stories taller than the vast front, looked to consist of basement and first-floor classrooms and a second and third floor auditorium, probably with a stage. I suspected the fourth floor contained a low-ceilinged gym.

The outer walls of the complex stood anywhere from ten to twenty feet inside a thick evergreen hedgerow that surrounded the entire place. Scaffolding, at various points piles of planks, and stacks of bricks all looking recently used, lay strewn about the open spaces between hedge and building.

We carried on a whispered conversation in the alley that separated the complex from the few houses on the rest of the block.

"The Lesbian Radicals from Hell meet in a church?" Scott asked.

"I don't think it's been a church for a while," I said. "All that construction shit scattered around smacks of rehabbers on the loose. That one corner where the streetlight hit the building full on showed all new window frames. No ugly grill work, no dirty opaque windows. No, this place had been fixed up, by somebody with a ton of money. Even you might need an investment group for this kind of shit." I eyed the exterior of the building carefully. "We're going exploring," I said.

"I hate that tone in your voice. It tells me you've had a moment of wild inspiration and daring. Usually it means mess, chaos, and deep shit up to our nipples.

"Jerry could be in there."

"Yeah," he conceded. "Then let's get the police."

"Are you serious? Even Frank Murphy, a cop we know who likes us, doesn't buy this shit. And while that Chicago cop may be gay, I don't trust him yet."

A dramatic sigh from Scott.

"Look," I said. "The place is absolutely dark. They've got to be holed up in some inside room. My guess is with all the construction crap still lying around, they're in the middle of renovating. We could explore for a week and not run into anybody. We'll hear them or see their lights long before they see us. Besides, Jerry could be in there. I'm going in."

"Alarm system?" Scott sounded resigned.

"If it's homemade, hopefully my training in Vietnam will be good enough to catch it before we trip it. If it's built in, that's why I have you along."

He's a mechanical genius. He fixes the decrepit appliances at my place, does repairs, major and minor, on my old Chevette that I kept even after I bought the truck this year. One time he installed an entire burglar alarm system around my place. I have absolute faith in his abilities.

We eased ourselves through the swaying bushes and hurried to crouch behind a stack of tarpaulin-covered two-by-fours. A short dash brought us to what must once have been the main entrance to the classrooms.

He punched my arm and pointed up. "That's the old alarm," he said indicating a foot-square box in the dim light.

I looked for holds for him to climb up. None that I could see.

"Boost me up," he muttered. He wound up standing on my shoulders. I braced myself against the side of the building to ease some of his weight. I'm six-foot-three and in great shape, but at six-four he's not a light burden. My shoulders seemed to endure several hours of this agony, while the rest of the universe probably felt a half a minute pass.

"Okay," he finally whispered.

I crouched down and he dismounted. He rubbed his hands on his jeans. "It's still connected," he announced, "but it hasn't been functional in years. The whole inside is rotted out." Around the building we crept, looking for an opening and more modern alarms.

Amazingly enough I found the alarm and managed to render it dysfunctional, in an odd way, without any assistance from Scott. The outside of the building had numerous abutments, decorative buttresses, cornices, along with nooks, crannies, and cubbyholes. Peeking around one of these I lost my footing, stumbled over a board, and with a soft crunch put my foot through the top of a box. I managed to accomplish this with only a slight thump from the box as my foot caved in the top. That is, if you didn't count the muffled laughter coming from immediately behind me. All right, it may have been funny, but was this the time to laugh?

I examined the box. Lettering on the outside indicated it contained parts for an alarm system. After a quick inspection I discovered three other boxes with the same lettering. So they'd never hooked up the damn thing. I'd still wrecked a good part of it. I extricated my leg from its trap and melted into the deeper shadows next to Scott.

"You're a big help," I muttered. Crouching in the shadows, I paused to reconnoiter. By this time we'd worked our way around three quarters of the building with no luck at finding an opening. I stood up and managed to bang my head on the bottom of an ancient metal stair-step fire escape. We'd seen several of them, although this was the only one that reached to within six feet of the ground. I whispered to him, "My bet is the place isn't wired at all."

"Good thing," Scott said. He tapped me on the shoulder and pointed. "While you were doing a ballet with the boxes, I found this."

In a dark recess behind a stack of bricks he'd found a boarded-up window.

"So what?" I said.

"It's loose," he said. He proceeded to ease the board back. We peered through the gap. No lights shone inside, but my eyes were fairly used to the dark by now. What I could see looked barren and empty. We slipped through the opening. It was the dim street-lights shining through all the wide new outside windows that made observation possible. An old blackboard on the wall told me this was a former classroom. As we crept forward we found openings, newly made, which would let at least two of the old classrooms, plus a washroom, become in the future one spacious and modern suite of rooms. The only appliances for the moment were the range, refrigerator, and dishwasher, all plunked in the middle of a soon-to-be-kitchen floor. We crept on. Heaps of two-by-fours, stacks of paint cans, and other construction paraphernalia lay in almost every room.

We had to move carefully to avoid stumbling over it. We must have covered over half the building before we heard or saw anything indicating current habitation. The place was a warren of rehabilitation waiting for those wealthy enough to be able to burrow in. The nave and choir loft had been turned into one dazzling series of interconnected lofts and staircases, presumably separate apartments or condos still to be walled off from one another. The whole thing had an Escher-like effect, all bathed in a soft glow of light let in by a vast skylight cut into the former church's roof.

In broad daylight it would take a platoon of men hours to explore the entire structure. Even then there were mysterious dangers, and huge possibilities of missing secret hiding places. I whispered this to Scott.

"Curb your imagination, big fella," he whispered. "Let's concentrate on what we can see and then get the hell out."

On the top floor of the back half of the building we encountered the darkest sections yet. No extra light leaked through to guide us. I listened intently but heard nothing. On hands and knees we crawled forward. I didn't want anymore klutzoid tripping. We came across a tiled floor and wide opening. I entered the space and let my hand rove up the wall. I felt a metal fixture. I guessed we were in the shower room section of the old locker room. We found a door opposite the one we entered. I eased it open a crack. Light again but still faint, but now for the first time I heard voices.

We crawled through this opening into a room filled with old lockers stacked in piles eight feet high. We inched across the floor to the farther door. A slit of light shone under it, a welcome beacon after the total blackout of minutes before. No question but that the voices came from behind this door. I eased it open a crack.

Soft lights in recessed sconces glowed around the old gymnasium. The half of the space closer to us was a wooden parquet floor. In places you could see the last flecks of paint marking the out-of-bounds lines. The low ceiling must have frustrated anybody trying to throw a full court pass.

Six people sat at the far end on folding chairs around two card tables pushed together. Beyond them, on the floor just to the right of a pair of double doors, sat a seventh person. Her bulk rested on a mattress. Eight of these lined the far walls. Piles of clothing and shelves made of bricks and boards separated each person's section. Cartons of what looked to be Chinese take-out sat on the card tables around which the six clustered. They spoke animatedly and without hurry. The figure on the floor drew my attention. She read by the light of a desk lamp that rested on the floor. She was the ugliest person I've ever seen. Her reddish-brown hair hung in lank strands to her shoulders. It looked as if she hadn't washed it yet this year. She wore a white sweat suit with frilly yellow flowers bursting on all sides. The sweat suit clung to the bulges of her figure in a very unflattering way. Her face had the requisite features but in the oddest shapes and sizes. Coke-bottle-thick glasses covered both eyes, over one of which she wore a black patch. Her lips were wide enough to drive a truck on. Her nose tilted off to the right side, as if it had been tweaked at an early age and left permanently off kilter. This had to be Stephanie, whom Monica had described when we'd talked to her after the break-in at the *Gay Tribune*.

Priscilla sat at the table. On her right sat a slender young woman in jeans and sweater. She was the only one who was the correct size to be the person we had followed. Next to her and opposite me sat a small woman in her mid-fifties in a flannel shirt and jeans. The next two women looked to be about college age. Both wore University of Chicago sweatshirts and faded jeans. The one in faded blue had blond hair moussed into a lengthy flat-top haircut. The woman in faded gray wore her long brown hair in a very fifties pony-tail. I couldn't make out the person whose back was toward me.

The general topic of conversation was their next move. A judge in downstate Illinois had recently ruled against a lesbian in a child custody case. They discussed various acts of violence against her person and property. They switched to an antiabortion group, the leader of which they suspected of being behind the fire bombing of an abortion clinic. Again they coolly discussed possible means of wreaking violet revenge on them. Nothing about a kidnapped twelve-year-old.

Suddenly the woman on the floor snapped her book shut and said, "Everybody stop."

Several people started to ask various forms of "What's up?"

"Hush!" the woman commanded. "We're being watched. I can feel it."

Shit, I said to myself. I wanted to close the door but didn't want to risk the slightest movement.

Priscilla snorted contemptuously. "Stephanie, you've been to one too many tarot card readings. I can't think of a safer place than this. We're—"

"There!" Stephanie screamed, pointing toward the door behind which we crouched. Chairs scraped back. Faces turned to us. In the instant before we turned to flee, I saw the face of the sixth person. I thought I recognized Prentice Dowalski, hustler extraodinaire.

No time for a second look. "Run!" I said as they started toward us.

We tried flying back the way we came. The abrupt appearance of a wall inches from my nose put an end to a mad dash. More cautiously but as quickly as possible we tried to move down and out.

Within seconds we'd lost our way. We managed to get out of the locker room area and down to the third floor, but neither of us could remember where the exit was for the next descent. Sounds of those following came sporadically. The darkness hampered them as much as it did us.

We came to a dead end and had to double back. We tried doors on every side. New apartments, dead ends with new appliances scattered around to bang into. The obstacles prevented anything like rapid progress. We came to the door through which we'd emerged from above. While Scott crept farther along, I listened a moment. The sound of squabbling voices came closer. I turned to realize I couldn't see Scott. I started off down the corridor.

"Here," he called, about twenty feet ahead and on the right. A window at the far end of the corridor let in enough light for me to see a door sway in the corridor.

"Come on," Scott urged.

I hurried forward. As I got to the door, I turned for a quick glance back. A female figure emerged from the staircase with a flashlight in her hand. The light crept toward us. We slammed the door and dashed forward. We found ourselves in another maze of passages. Sounds of pursuit nearing forced us to dangerous speed. Through the uncertain light we blundered and stumbled. Finally we emerged on a balcony overlooking a vast space. Above, the new skylight told me we'd entered the nave of the old church. We had sufficient light to see our way down from the balcony. Two sets of steps on opposite sides led into the abyss below. We heard feet pounding behind us. I glanced down. We could see each level of the unfinished lofts as they branched out. A quick look showed no sign of anyone below us cutting off our retreat. We'd have to descend into the maze.

"This way," we told each other. Seconds later I realized he'd gone down the other steps. Before I could try retracing my way, the door we'd come through burst open. I turned and flew down the stairs. On the second level I almost boxed myself in, taking a wrong turn into a master bedroom. I reemerged and glanced quickly around. On the level above me and across the gaping chasm, I saw a flashlight bobbing erratically from side to side. For an instant the light caught Scott.

"Get him!" a voice screamed.

The vast room echoed now with shouting voices and thundering footsteps. Above me on my side, I heard slower pursuit. No light shone on this side.

I rushed to my right and found a grand staircase. I hurried

down, then paused at the bottom. I couldn't see an opening that led up to meet up with Scott.

"Run!" I heard him shout. He was on a series of steps a level and a half above me. "I'll meet you outside." He gestured frantically and disappeared. Despite his words I tried desperately to find a way to get up to the other side. In the precious moments I used on this task my pursuers closed in.

"Hold it, asshole."

I turned. The heavy-set woman who'd been reading on the floor stood at the head of a contingent of three, ten feet in front of me. They blocked the way to a series of steps down. "We got one," she called out.

I dashed straight for the closest woman. She flinched for a second, but her foot darted out in a well-aimed karate kick. I'd had similar training and managed to deflect the blow with my right arm. It still hurt like hell, but I managed to shove her as I dove past. She fell into the other two, and I rushed for the flight of stairs behind them.

On the ground floor now, I looked for any kind of exit. The doors were locked tight. This section had all new windows. Each had double-thick safety glass that you'd need a truck to burst through. I was far too lost to be able to find the way we'd come in the first time. Behind me I heard several loud screams and a yodel of triumph. Had they captured Scott? I turned a corner and came upon a pile of window casements. I'd stumbled on the spot where the workmen had stopped putting in new windows that day. I gave the old window a swift look-see. Old and opaque. I picked up a board and smashed the glass. Only rusted metal grating stood between me and freedom. Bracing my arms on the window sides, I pounded my foot against it. It gave on the second thunk; with the third, it clattered to the ground. I jumped through; dropped three feet to the ground, and ran. I didn't go far; I stopped at the hedge to look back. The wind howled around me, but as yet no rain or snow fell.

A face appeared at the opening I'd created. After searching

looks left and right she disappeared. I stayed still and caught my breath. Then light appeared at the window. I saw Priscilla's face as she flashed the beam around the building's exterior. I crouched unmoving in my hiding place. The beam couldn't penetrate the thick evergreen hedge. Moments later the light disappeared.

I spent the next thirty minutes in two painstaking circles around the outside of the building, looking for Scott. I halted when I realized he could be doing the same thing. We could circle each other endlessly. I waited. Time crept by at an achingly slow pace. No sounds came from inside or outside the building. After fifteen minutes, I decided to go back in. Scott could be captured, trapped, hiding, anything. So far they hadn't called the cops. Assuming they were the Lesbians for Freedom and Dignity, they'd be reluctant to draw police attention to themselves, especially if they were in residence illegally. For similar reasons, I wasn't eager to call the cops.

Carefully I returned to our original point of entry. Slowly I eased back the board and listened intently. No sound. I crawled through the opening and jumped the two feet to the floor. Instantly bright light shone in my face. Powerful hands gripped me from all sides. Wrenching my arms painfully behind me, they dragged me through the complex. We met Priscilla in the center of the old church under the massive skylight.

She took the flashlight from the one called Stephanie and shone it in my face.

"Macho Mason," she sneered. She waved the flashlight at the two others gathered on her right. "I told you he'd come back for his pal."

"Where's Scott?" I asked.

She pointed. "Up. We've heard him, but we haven't been able to catch him. We've got the exits covered. He can't get down without getting caught. We figured you'd be back to look for him. We found your entrance and waited."

They led me back to the ground level of the loft room. One of the women pulled the belt from her pants and used it to secure my hands behind me. She stepped back. Priscilla placed the flashlight ten feet away on the railing for the first flight of stairs to the first loft. The diffused light showed three women and no Prentice.

"What'd you hear upstairs?" Stephanie said.

"Fuck you," I said.

She kicked me in the nuts. I doubled over and slumped to the ground, groaning in agony.

"Answer or you get more of that," she commanded.

Gasping for breath, I waited for the waves of pain and nausea to subside. Breathing under control I asked, "Where's my nephew?"

Stephanie had a gravelly whiskey voice, whether natural or acquired, I couldn't tell. She said, "We ask the questions."

"We took him," Priscilla said.

I struggled to my feet. "If he's harmed in any way, I'll kill you."

"Do that," she said calmly and gave a ripple of laughter. "We've been calling your place to give you a message, but you haven't been home. Leaving a kidnap message on an answering machine is stupid, and Carpenter's number is unlisted."

"Why'd you kidnap Jerry?" I asked.

"To stop your meddling. We don't need you guys snooping around. As it turns out, our fears were quite well founded. Here you are, and you've heard too much. You're forcing us to unusual action. We can't keep you, and we can't let you go. If we have you, your nephew is expendable."

A tremendous bellow split the silence. I looked up in time to see a shape hurtling down. I leaped back. Something landed with a tremendous crash halfway between Priscilla and me. Fragments flew in every direction. I scrambled to the railing, twisted around, and clutched the flashlight in my tied hands. I flicked it off and ran for the stairs. I heard the women begin to follow. Another bellow split the air. I stopped and looked up. A massive object tipped at a crazy angle from the top loft. I dashed up the stairs. A second later another crash sounded behind me. From the top of the landing I looked down. Halfway down, the stairs no longer existed. The women at the bottom shouted in frustration. Priscilla put a quick stop to that. She issued commands. The group below scattered. One raced up the stairs on the other side of the vast space. The other hurried through other openings to pursue paths I couldn't be aware of. I scrambled upward, careful of my balance with my hands still tied. Two thirds of the way up I met Scott coming down. It took only seconds to untie me. We could only use the flashlight sparingly for fear it would alert pursuers to our presence. Even with its help, we wound up in the locker room again.

"Shit," I said.

Sounds of pursuit came from the corridor behind. We hurried through the locker room and into the gym. Empty. We raced across the floor and through the double doors. Construction materials lay scattered about a wide entranceway. To the left, the corridor ended in two opaque windows. Across from us was a solid brick wall. To the right a wide staircase led down. We paused at the top of the stairs. Voices drifted from below. We raced back to the doors.

"We could fight them," Scott said.

"I don't like the odds. Remember, Monica said they've all had special training in self-defense." While we gasped these words at each other, we wedged planks against the doors. Someone shoved them from the other side. The planks budged but held. Then I heard the sounds of people hammering against the doors.

"That won't hold long," Scott said.

"I haven't seen any evidence of weapons," I said, "but I don't want to take chances. They sounded pretty bloodthirsty earlier. We'll fight if we have to."

Scott ran to the windows. I rushed to the top of the stairs. I heard angry voices, then Stephanie's overriding the others. "Priscilla's not here. I'm using the gun on them if we get there before she does."

The sound of smashing glass caused me to turn. Scott had a plank, accomplishing the same thing I had done earlier. I saw the last shards of glass fall outward. I hurried over. Drenching rain driven by a howling wind greeted my vision. The storm had taken a piss-poor time to break. Outside the window, one of the rusted fire escapes we'd seen earlier offered us our only chance. At one point some fool, to keep intruders out, had placed mesh screening over the outer window, violating fire codes and rendering the fire escape useless. Two blasts of the timber in Scott's powerful arms, and the rusted metal flew into the night. No point in looking back. I couldn't remember exactly, but I hoped this was the fire escape that held together all the way to the ground. I chose not to think of the alternatives. Scott threw the board aside and scrambled onto the metal planking. It squeaked ominously. Quickly I joined him. The structure groaned. I examined the massive bolts holding stairs to the building. Not reassuring. The ones still in place seemed to be secured mostly by rust and a prayer. I didn't think about what would happen if they gave way.

We stood five stories above the ground. Below, hidden in darkness between folds of the building, was the ground and safety. I still couldn't tell if the damn thing reached all the way down or not. Rain pelted into my eyes and washed over my chin.

Scott led the way. Our feet clattered on the railings. Halfway down I heard voices above. We rushed faster. On the third landing Scott stumbled. We collided and fell. A shot rang out.

"Motherfucker!" Scott swore. We untangled ourselves and sped earthward. They fired only the one shot. The wild dash and my fear made it tentative, but I thought I heard Priscilla's voice berating someone. Probably Stephanie, the gun wielder.

Closer to the bottom now, I could see that the fire escape ended fifteen feet from the ground. We paused at the edge. I looked up. So far no one had followed. The structure trembled and groaned under us.

"Now what?" Scott gasped.

"We shut our eyes, click our heels together three times, and say there's no place like home."

"I could do without any Kansas shit right now," he said. The fire escape groaned ominously.

"Turn backwards," I commanded, "grab hold of the bottom rung, get your legs over, and let yourself dangle. Swing out hard, jump, and hit the ground rolling. That'll distribute your weight. Less chance of injury."

"Right. You first. I'll watch."

I turned around, got my feet over the last step, grabbed hold of a railing, and backed up. I eased my knees, then my torso over the edge. For a second my hands slipped. I grasped the railing, swung once and again, pushed off, and hit the ground rolling. I leaped to my feet. I watched Scott duplicate my efforts, moving backward and swinging out. His feet dangled four feet above me. He swung out once. The rail snapped on his back swing and he fell.

He landed on me. We lay, limbs entangled for several startled seconds. Moments later we were on our feet and running. An angry rumble from the building behind stopped me in my tracks. I watched the ancient fire escape rattle, then crumble in slow stages to the ground. Scott grabbed my arm. "Let's go!" he shouted. We ran.

We didn't stop until we'd gotten back to the parking lot in front of the Burger King we passed earlier just west of Clark Street. I wanted to call Frank Murphy before we called the Chicago police. After all, we had entered illegally. We used the pay phone to call the River's Edge police station. Frank Murphy wasn't on duty. I got his home number from directory assistance and called.

It was just after one. A very sleepy Frank answered on the sixth ring. When I got it through to him about the kidnapping, he came awake enough to tell me to wait there. He'd handle it.

We huddled under the overhang outside the restaurant. Our winter coats had kept out the worst of the rain, but drops fell from my nose and chin as I tried to squeeze the dampness out of my hair.

Ten minutes later a cop car pulled up. We got in the back

seat. Our explanation took endless moments before they drove to the church. Maybe they needed to make sure our story confirmed Frank's.

At the church the cops delayed again. We urged a dramatic frontal assault. They claimed they has to wait for backup and permission. We argued about it, intermixed with their fascination with meeting Scott Carpenter. I was never more frustrated with his fame. He too tried to get them to move, but to no avail.

By the time someone of sufficient rank showed up, it'd be too late. I knew they'd be gone. Frank drove up a few minutes after the first contingent had entered the building. We walked in with him. The rain had stopped, and the wind had changed direction, now driving with a cold roar out of the northwest. Through the many levels and corridors we saw lights flickering. When we got to the top floor, it was as I feared: no one, not even the remains of dinner on the table. All the clothes and sleeping bags had disappeared. The only proofs of our story that remained were the various signs of destruction and the now-barren card tables and chairs in the middle of the gym floor.

8

They searched, and we waited. Just past two, Frank found us poking into obscure corners in a sub-basement. Early in the search they'd found the lights the construction workers used. These cast feeble glares at random intervals.

Frank had Monica Verlaine with him. "This is the owner," he said.

We explained that we'd met. Monica wore a fur coat open to reveal a purple evening dress.

Monica claimed not to know the women had been using the place for trysting. "Priscilla must have learned about this place and my ownership from records at the newspaper. She'd know work orders and times." She denied all knowledge of their activities. I'd begun to trust her, but now I wasn't so sure.

Frank said, "They found traces in the gym. The police believe your story."

"They claimed they had Jerry," I said. "I want them caught."

Monica said, "Mr. Mason and Mr. Carpenter, I asked you to look into Father Sebastian's death. I'm sorry to have involved your family. Believe me, I had no wish for this to happen." Her sultry voice dropped a level. "I apologize. If I could put an end to all this, I would."

Paul Turner, the gay Chicago cop, walked into the room. We'd moved to the entryway of the first-floor apartment.

We explained the situation to him, emphasizing Priscilla's admission of the kidnapping. Scott hadn't seen Prentice, so he couldn't swear to his presence. I was sure it was him.

Just before three, we left. On the stoop in the cold wind, as we finished buttoning our coats against the storm, Turner said, "I find your suspicions about the priest's death more credible for the moment. Your problem is why and how." He turned at the bottom of the steps, "You're going to question Prentice. So am I. You'd better come along."

We rode in an unmarked police car to Bruce's Halfway There Bar. I knew it had a late license and would still be open. Prentice saw us walk in and immediately began backing toward the rear exit. I stopped him before he could get to the door beyond the jukebox in back and dragged him to the front of the bar by the belt and shirt collar. The few patrons on this midweek stormy winter night had scattered at the first sign of trouble.

Paul Turner had a baritone voice. He spoke slowly and softly in his harsh South Side Chicago accent. "Let him go," he said quietly and forcefully.

I took my hands off him. Prentice shook himself, straightened the collar of his shirt, and pulled his sleeves taut.

Turner introduced himself and showed his star. "You aren't under arrest, but I'd like to check on your whereabouts tonight."

"I want my lawyer," Prentice said.

No matter how patiently Turner asked, that's all Prentice said. I grabbed for him when my frustration reached the boiling point. Turner stopped me. We left soon after. On the sidewalk Turner said, "We don't beat confessions out of people anymore. I know he's a whore. He knows he has to watch his step. He's a pro at being arrested. I can tell. When all they do is ask for their lawyer, they've been through it before. If you're thinking of going back after I'm gone, don't. Let the police handle this."

He got in his car and drove off.

Seconds later we were back in the bar. Prentice had the

phone in one hand. He saw us and quickly hung up. He edged toward the rear. I glided to the back to block any exit. Scott turned the lock on the front door to prevent any interruption.

"Get serious, you guys." He stood in front of the cash register halfway down the bar. "You can't do nothing to me." His eyes darted back and forth from one to the other of us. "I wasn't there. Honest."

Scott lunged for him. Prentice grabbed a bottle from the shelf behind the bar and smashed it on top of the cash register. He held the resulting jagged edge toward us.

"I'll use this." He flourished the bottle as he moved closer to me.

As he neared, I made my move. Seconds later the sleeve of my leather winter coat lay in tatters, but I had my hand around his throat and the back of his head up against the wall. "You motherfucker. Where's my nephew?"

He said something like "*Gaklumphack.*"

I eased the pressure. He tried a few feeble kicks. I reapplied pressure. He stopped struggling and concentrated on breathing.

"He can't talk if you kill him," Scott pointed out.

Slowly I released him. He slumped to the floor, choking and gasping for breath.

Scott got him a glass of ice water and knelt down next to him.

Prentice sat on the floor with his back up against the bar and accepted the water gratefully. He slurped for a moment, choked, spluttered, then swallowed. When his color returned to normal, Scott said, "I'm not the nice guy in a good-cop bad-cop deal here. I want to hurt you as much as Tom does."

Prentice's scared look, which had begun to pass, returned in a rush.

"We know you were there," I said. "We only want to know where Jerry is. You gave it away when you tried to take off as soon as you saw us. We'll beat the information out of you. Slowly and carefully, if necessary. We won't kill you, but it'll hurt a lot, trust me."

Still on the floor, Prentice looked up at me. I'd taken a seat on one side of a booth directly across from him. The aisle was narrow so our feet were only inches apart. Scott crouched next to him.

Prentice let out a disgusted sigh. "Why should I protect those bitches? They're nuts anyway." He crossed his ankles and looked at us in turn. "They think they're part of some vast conspiracy to overthrow the paternalistic underpinnings of western civilization." He gave a harsh laugh. "If they're lucky, they've got twenty people in their group nationwide, and that's an optimistic count."

"Do they really blow up places?" Scott asked.

"One. A place in San Francisco, and that almost didn't work. Then their explosives person had a fight with Priscilla over the name of the group. She thought it didn't sound militant enough. This was when Priscilla was out in San Francisco last month."

"Who's done the other bombings?" Scott asked.

"They don't know. Nut cases? Priscilla thinks other groups saw the sympathy and the donations that poured in after the first bombing, and now they're doing it themselves to get their own publicity. The problem they didn't expect is that all kinds of nut groups began calling the media to take credit. Donations dried up."

"Where's Jerry?" I asked.

"I don't know," he said. "They didn't discuss him while I was there."

Even after seventeen years of listening to teenage liars, I couldn't tell if this was the truth or not. Turner was right. The guy was a pro.

Scott reached out and grabbed the crotch of Prentice's tight jeans and squeezed. The kid screamed in agony. "I'm going to ruin your business forever, motherfucker, if you're lying. You *sure* you don't know?" He squeezed tighter. Prentice yelped, groaned, swatted feebly with one hand. Sweat poured freely down his red face. "I . . . don't . . . know," he managed to gasp out.

116

Scott let go. The kid rolled on his side, his hands over his crotch. Scott knelt next to him, turned him on his back, and got his feet flat on the ground with his knees up. Prentice's breathing returned to normal in a few minutes.

"Motherfucking bastards," he said.

Scott shrugged. Prentice crawled to his feet, using the bar for support. He summoned a few shreds of dignity. "I have to close up," he said. He staggered toward the back of the bar.

At the front door I turned to ask, "Did you know Sebastian was HIV positive?"

He looked startled. "No. Guess it's a good thing he refused to have sex with me the times I offered."

"What were you doing there tonight?" Scott asked.

"Priscilla is my sister." He turned his back on us, binged open the cash register, and began counting the money.

Back at Scott's place, as we crawled into his bed, we decided our next step had to be more background on Sebastian. Finding Jerry and the truth about Sebastian's death were inextricably linked in my mind. Turner's questions made sense: why and how? We'd concentrated on running around and talking to scared or powerful people. Why and how would lead to the who. I wanted to talk Monica's source more than ever.

Just as I was about to fall asleep, I jerked suddenly wide awake. "How did you know I wouldn't get killed when you dropped that thing from so high up?"

He mumbled into his pillow. He normally falls asleep on his stomach. I usually nod off lying on my back. Snuggling after sex can lead to alterations in these habits.

"How'd you know?" I said, propping myself up on one elbow and nudging his shoulder.

He lifted his head an inch from the pillow and opened one eye. He said, "I aimed." His head resumed its initial position.

"You what?" Another nudge. "How do you aim from four stories up?"

This time he got both eyes open. "Am I the highest-paid

117

pitcher in baseball?" He didn't wait for an answer. "Of course I am. That's my job. I throw things at a target. I don't miss."

Less than satisfactory as answers go and hardly reassuring, and not what I wanted to hear, but before I could think of a question or make a protest, he turned on his side, leaned over, and pulled me close. He nestled my head onto his chest. I felt the thick blond fur there against my cheek. He stroked my back. We talked about love and danger, and then had a bout of passionate sex, and then fell asleep in each other's arms.

First thing in the morning, tired from a much-too-short night's sleep, I called Glen to fill him in. Then I phoned Kurt to check on strike and negotiations progress. He was at school leading the picketing so I talked to his wife, Beth. She asked about Jerry. After all these years, she was as good a friend to us as Kurt was. She told me to forget school and take care of family business.

At eight-thirty Monica Verlaine called. "Neil gave me your number. I've got my source with me. We can be at your place in thirty minutes."

At nine the doorman called from downstairs to announce them.

Monica wore a navy blue suit with matching shoes and purse, of course. She'd added a gold ring with an enormous black star sapphire set in it.

Her source had to be in his nineties. He wore the black pants, shirt, suit coat, and white Roman collar with stiff dignity and pride. He shook our hands firmly. His bald head had a circle of gray fringe.

We sat at the butcher-block kitchen table. Scott put on the coffee the old gentleman had requested as refreshment. Monica introduced him as Father Gilbert Stuart. "He lives in the cathedral rectory. He's agreed to help us."

The old man spoke in a soft tenor, a hint of wheeze and crackle well under control. "I knew Father Sebastian in the seminary. The other priests ignore me in my retirement,

118

although a few still remember. Lately, the activities of the priests have bothered me. When Monica told me about your nephew, I knew I had to speak. Something is wrong. I love the Church, it's been good to me, but there has to be a limit to what its priests can get away with."

"Why not go to the police?" I asked.

"Monica convinced me you would be best. Discretion is of the highest importance, and you have it."

Scott gave him his coffee. He spent some time adding sugar and cream, testing it several times to make sure it was to his liking. He looked up as he gave the brew a few last stirs.

"That's one of the advantages of being ninety-two," he said. "You can put any damn thing in your coffee you want, you can eat anything you want, and the damn doctors just marvel at you like some icon."

He took a sip of coffee and smiled appreciatively.

"You can also be as honest as you want. You need help in solving this murder. Let me tell you about myself first. You need to be able to trust me. First of all, I'm gay."

Scott and I stirred in our chairs and looked at each other. Monica took this news impassively.

He told his story between sips of coffee. He'd discovered his sexuality when he was in his twenties, long before anyone even dreamed of a gay rights movement. He knew Henry Gerber back in the twenties in Chicago when Gerber and a group of other men formed one of the first gay rights groups in the country. "We were all extremely closeted. No one used last names. Being part of it was horribly daring for a priest at the time."

Henry Gerber founded the Society for Human Rights, a group chartered by the State of Illinois on December 24, 1924. They published a paper called *Friendship and Freedom*. Their activities quickly led to trouble with the police. A number of people in the group, including Gerber, were arrested without a warrant. Eventually the charges were dismissed, but Gerber wound up losing his job.

"Of course, no one knew I was a priest. I wasn't arrested.

When I found out about the trouble, I never went near any of them again. That was so sad and so cowardly."

Then, in his first parish assignment on Chicago's West Side, he'd fallen in love with an assistant pastor a few years older than himself. Amazingly, their relationship blossomed into a lifelong attachment.

"We loved each other very deeply. Of course, we had to be exceptionally careful. It's bad for gay priests now, but then it would have been ghastly. We'd meet in secret. We had sex only rarely, but it was all the more passionate for that. We got transferred to different parishes, but we managed to keep our relationship quiet and exclusive all those years. We were faithful more from circumstances than from choice. He died three years ago."

After working in parishes for fifteen years, Father Stuart had been assigned to various positions in the seminary program, finally being put in charge. He'd known Sebastian well. "He and John Smith, whom you have already met, were incredibly close. They did everything together. I had to warn them several times to be more discreet. It was dangerous to form 'particular friendships' in those days. It still is."

Sebastian and Smith took part in much of the civil rights activity in the early Sixties. As newly ordained priests they'd both gone to Selma, Alabama, to take part in the marches.

He looked at his empty coffee cup. Scott refilled it. As Stuart performed his rituals with the liquid he continued. "Monica, of course, has told me everything." He sipped coffee and coughed. "You should have seen the cathedral rectory these past weeks. I've seen the same kind of activity when a priest molests a child: secret meetings, everybody knowing a little piece of distorted fact, and nobody really knowing anything. It's like a hive of old queens trying to know all and be discreet at the same time."

It turned out that the new cardinal hated gay people. Even more, he wanted absolutely no publicity about priests testing positive for, having, or dying of AIDS. The hierarchy was always hideously worried about "scandalizing the faithful," buzz words like "national security" for covering up when priests or politicians broke the law or in general screwed up. "Smith is in charge of the cover-up. You wouldn't believe the clout the church still has in this town."

If it was AIDS or murder, Father Stuart went on to explain, he wanted the truth to come out.

"Were Sebastian and Smith actually lovers back then?" I asked.

"You ask a question I've thought about a great deal. They were both attractive boys and very popular. Everybody liked them. They'd both have gone far. Smith dropped the relationship a year or so after they were ordained. I never knew why. He advanced far, as many of us thought he would. He could have his own diocese someday as bishop. Sebastian never compromised his principles. He kept marching for every cause. He upset parishioners and priests. I wish I'd been as brave as he was. They couldn't keep him from being a pastor, but he knew he'd never advance much further in the system, and it didn't seem to bother him."

He took a long sip of his coffee and stared out the window over the lake. "Were they lovers? No, I don't think so. If I had to make a guess, I'd say it was because Sebastian demanded more than Smith could give. John Smith is a good man, a fine priest, but he has his limitations. Sebastian had his faults too. As a seminarian, he could drive you nuts with his intensity and commitment."

"This is all hypocritical bullshit," I said.

Father Stuart smiled softly. He was the first priest we'd met who didn't indulge in condescension and put-down games, two skills they must have classes in for the modern Catholic seminary.

Monica blew out a long stream of smoke and eyed us all carefully.

"You think being a priest and gay is hypocritical?" The priest's question came out softly and reasonably.

Scott nodded.

"Do you have any idea of how many priests are gay?"

We all shook our heads.

"Some estimates go as high as fifty percent. I can tell you from my own observations of three decades in formation work that it is probably higher than that." He told us that most gay priests hide the fact from others and from themselves. That lots of Catholic boys, discovering they didn't like girls, translated that into believing they'd be able to cope with celibacy with no problem, and thought they had a calling. "They do decent work for a number of years, but eventually most of them begin to figure it out. Often it's too late to leave. Running a parish leaves you woefully unqualified for any jobs in the real world." Father Stuart told us that when you listened to priests talk about life in the "real world" it was often quite sad. They would sneer at the strivings of their parishioners and yet be fearful of ever leaving the protection of Holy Mother Church. For the older ones it was worse. To leave in your fifties or sixties with no pension behind you left a man to face years of poverty-stricken retirement. "So they stay and they're miserable. The alcoholism rate among priests is appalling."

"Why not just come out?" Scott asked. "What could the church do to them? From what I heard it's impossible to defrock somebody once he's in."

"They're afraid of the same thing many of us are afraid of: rejection, loss of status, fear of reprisal, loss of current assignment and future promotions, loss of respect, scandal—and then there's all that child molestation myth shit."

The profanity from the old priest surprised me. He took another sip of coffee and said, "What I'm telling you isn't a big secret. Most of it's in James G. Wolf's book *Gay Priests*. You should read it."

"I guess," Scott said.

Stuart pointed at Scott. "It's very much like what would happen if word got into the press that you were gay. You'd still be a superb baseball player, but the hassles would be enormous."

"The anticipation of discrimination can often cause more problems than the discrimination itself," Monica said. "A guy named Ross wrote an article about it you should read."

Stuart said, "I'm afraid our new Bishop is only going to make things worse. Of course, he fits the classic mold of the self-denying homosexual who is the worst enemy of gay people. He's the type who would prosecute them the most eagerly."

Monica said, "Sebastian was the only priest I've ever met who could balance his celibacy and yet be sensitive, emotionally responsive, and happy at the same time. That kind of balance is rare in a gay priest. Most are so unhappy."

Do you know anything about Sebastian's family?" I asked.

"I believe they're all dead," Stuart said.

Monica said, "He rarely mentioned them. He did say once that he came from a family of Episcopalians. He converted while in high school. He said his family had a major problem with his being a priest."

"My suggestion as a place for you to start is another interview with Bishop Smith," Stuart said. "You've gotten in once before. He can be very difficult. I'd like to help, but I'm just an old fart he'd ignore, and I don't want to be revealed as your source of information. I may be old and safe, but I'd like to continue to be of use. Revealed, I can do you very little good."

They left and we called the cathedral rectory. Smith wasn't home. We could try the chancery office. We called, but Father Smith was unavailable. We decided to try barging into the diocesan offices and demanding an audience. I wasn't about to put up with some ecclesiastical bullshit.

The diocesan offices took up the bottom floors of a high rise on the corner of Michigan Avenue and Ontario. We parked at Scott's building and walked over. The wind and rain of the night before had given way to a cool crisp morning. Without a covering of snow for reinforcement, the arctic blast had a harder time getting a solid grip on the city.

We arrived at the chancery shortly after one. We used Scott's name to move secretaries and the mountain of bureaucracy to action. Even the Catholic Church was susceptible to the power of fame and name dropping. All business came to a halt as friend called to friend. Father Smith discovered us amid a horde of adoring fans, both male and female.

When Smith arrived, priests and civilians gave him wary looks and moved quickly back to their assigned tasks. Moments later he guided us through empty halls to a third-floor office. The room contained a massive desk flanked by the American flag on the left and the papal gold and white on the right. The wall on the left had three enlarged, framed photographs. In each we saw Smith with, starting from the door, the pope, the president, and the mayor of Chicago. The other walls were barren beige. The carpeting was light brown. In front of the massive oak desk sat two deep maroon leather chairs. We each sank into one. He took his seat in the massive swivel chair behind the desk.

He smiled benignly, steepled his fingers, and placed them under his chin. The light from the windows behind him created the godlike effect he wanted.

Smith began some pleasant, innocuous comment.

I cut in quietly. "You and Sebastian were lovers thirty years ago."

The maddening smile went on. "And if we were, so what?" he murmured. "Are you going to send out a press release? No one would print it. No one cares. His soon-to-be-cardinal eminence doesn't care. Believe me, he sympathizes completely."

"How can he be sympathetic and justify closing down Faith?" I asked.

Smith spread his hands palm up. "He can be gay and still close it down. Rules are rules. Rome has spoken. If you can't buy the program, get out."

"You've had it both ways," I said.

"I've done a great deal, in my small way, for gay Catholics. When Faith got thrown out of their church, I got them all their supplies: vestments, chalices, wine, hosts. My conscience is clear." The hands returned to their accustomed place under his chin.

"Sebastian was HIV positive," I said.

"Yes, I know." For the first time a slight crack appeared in his smug exterior.

"Did that bother you?" I asked. "Supposedly you were still close friends."

"We were," he said. His eyes got misty. "But it was too late for me to do anything about it."

I let his wistful words fade to silence. Finally, he shook himself and turned cold eyes to us. "What else do you dare to ask?"

"Why did you involve Father Clarence in all this?"

"As head troubleshooter for the diocese, I take an interest in every priest who might cause scandal for the faithful. In an excess of guilt he might confess all. I had to prevent that. Perhaps I was excessively harsh with the young man."

"Is this the way you handle all the young priests under your care?" Scott said. "You become their 'special friend'? Although Clarence strikes me as relentlessly heterosexual."

"I'm afraid he is. Attractive he might be, but I've never touched him—as I never touched any other young priest."

"If you were so close to Sebastian, why aren't you concerned about finding the cause of his death?" I asked.

He smiled wanly. "He was already dying." We sat in silence for moments. Suddenly Smith sat up straighter in his chair. "Because I knew of his antibody status, I presumed his death was connected to some aspect of the syndrome." He cleared his throat. "Besides which, one of the major roles here is to prevent what we call 'scandal to the faithful.'" He explained that to all but the incredibly stupid, this catch phrase meant the church was covering up another fuck-up. I didn't tell him we already knew this. He went on to say that, as the AIDS epidemic spread, more and more priests had been dying of the disease. Various dioceses managed to conceal the true cause of the deaths. However, word had leaked out, and some cases and reports had gotten into the press. "We can't have that kind of publicity. Gay priests and AIDS. Supposedly the pope was furious about the whole issue. We've got strict orders. No publicity about gay priests, with or without AIDS. I can tell you that cover-ups in this city are quite possible."

"We need the autopsy report," I said.

"Actually, you don't." The benign smile returned. "The report states he died of natural causes. No examination of any kind occurred. You'll get no help there. People value their jobs too much to blab to you gentlemen. But in this case there is nothing to blab. Nobody found anything, because nobody looked."

I wanted to grab the thick gold chain that held his heavy gold cross and wrap it tightly around his stupid smug throat.

"You don't care that somebody may have killed him?" Scott asked.

He had the decency to look thoughtful before he gave a cold no. We asked if he knew of any current problems, boyfriends, or priests Sebastian was close to. We got simple no's. Minutes later, we left.

Before working out at Scott's, I called Glen and Jeannette. Glen's voice had lost all the bounce and verve it normally had. I spoke what words of encouragement I could. We'd been exercising for an hour, and I'd just finished my third set of eight chin-ups, when the phone rang. I grabbed a towel from the pile by the Universal weight machine, then hurried to the phone on the wall. I wiped off sweat as I picked up the receiver.

It was Mildred Weber from St. Joseph's rectory. "We have to see you boys." She wouldn't tell me what for on the phone, but we could come to their home right after dark.

Feeling only slightly ridiculous, but on the off chance they really knew something, we drove to the suburbs. Across the street from the Webers' the rectory blazed with light. We found their house completely dark. Climbing the stairs I felt uneasy. I had my hand raised to knock when the door jerked open. A hand reached out and yanked me in. "Hurry," an elderly voice whispered. Scott jumped in behind me.

Mildred put her finger to her lips. The dimness made close observation difficult, but I could see overstuffed furniture covered with lace doilies cluttering the room.

She dragged us to the front picture window and knelt on the floor next to Harriet. Mildred motioned for us to join them. Down we crouched. Between the closed drapes and the window pane was a two-inch gap.

"We always watch from here," Mildred whispered.

I looked and saw the lit rectory. I detected no human movement.

"What's going on?" Scott asked.

Mildred explained without taking her eyes off the rectory. She said, "It's been going on all afternoon. First that awful Bishop Smith showed up."

"Father Sebastian introduced us once," Harriet said. "I didn't trust him from the first minute, did I?"

They did their nod routine.

Smith had stayed an hour. Constance quit in a screaming fit around four. Smith left soon after. Clarence snarled at Mildred and Harriet. They left, directionless and at a loss, without even preparing supper, something they'd always done. Since then a woman had driven up. From the description I guessed her to be Clarence's wife. In the middle of her visit a small moving truck had driven up. They spent a half hour moving Father Clarence's things out of the house. They'd driven off twenty minutes before we drove up.

Fascinating as all this might have been, I didn't care about Father Clarence unless he was part of the kidnapping solution. He'd lied to us, but even if Smith told us lies too, I'd begun to suspect Clarence was an innocent man caught in a web far beyond his own comprehension. He had enough problems of his own.

After watching five more minutes of no movement, I said, "Why did you call us?"

They eased their creaking bones off the floor and drew us deeper into the house. A swinging door led from a dining room into the kitchen. Before turning on the lights, they pulled all the shades and shut the drapes.

Once my eyes adjusted to the light I gazed on a room that looked exactly like a maiden aunt's kitchen should, from the metal canisters with ingredient labels on the outside to the embroidered *God bless our home* framed plaque. A filled glass cookie jar sat on a corner of the counter next to the refrigerator. The room smelled of fresh bread and musty old wood mixed with spices on the tip of recognition.

They seated us. A plate of cookies, fresh bread, and corn muffins appeared, along with tall glasses of milk. At first we tried saying no thanks. It was like trying to refuse your grandmother. We ate and sipped and waited. When we were sufficiently fed, they brought out their revelation.

Harriet got out a stepstool from the pantry, climbed it, and pulled a stack of mail from the top shelf of the cupboard over the sink.

"This is Father Sebastian's mail," she said.

I raised an eyebrow.

"We didn't steal it," Harriet said.

"We've been in charge of sorting mail at the rectory for twenty years," Mildred added. "Constance and Father Clarence tried to take the job away from us, but Father Sebastian came to our rescue."

They hadn't known what to do with the dead priest's mail. No one seemed to care when they asked, so they'd kept it and brought it home every night.

"It was my idea to show it to you," Harriet said. "Like those detectives on TV. You're so young and handsome, and you were so polite last time. We wanted to help you. We thought this might be a clue."

There must have been thirty envelopes, all open. I asked about this.

"Father Sebastian trusted us. We'd open each piece of mail, examine it, and decide on its importance. We placed it in separate piles on his desk every afternoon. We'd been doing it for ten years. It saved him time."

"Plus you thought you might try a little detective work yourselves," Scott suggested.

They nodded. "But it didn't do us any good. We couldn't find anything important," Harriet said. "Then we thought of you. And you were such nice boys. We wanted to see you again." She smiled shyly. "We forgot to get Mr. Carpenter's autograph."

I felt odd looking through a dead man's mail. It seemed illegal, or at least indecent. This gave me pause for a second. If anything here gave us a clue to finding Jerry, I wasn't concerned about esoteric legal points.

The four of us sat around the Formica-top table on plastic-covered chairs. The women watched as Scott and I divided the stacks. I started with very little hope. They'd seen too many TV shows. My stack had a few bills, a lot of junk mail, and a personal letter from a former parishioner now living in California. I examined everything carefully. The letter was innocuous and pleasant enough from someone unaware of tragedy. The bills showed no pattern. A few meals on his VISA charge at suburban restaurants didn't reveal anything. The MasterCard bill showed some purchases at a men's clothing store in the past month. It could have been socks and underwear. No singular fact leap out to reveal a hidden life.

Scott sat leafing through a small stack of canceled checks. He had the other mail sitting to his left. He slowly began separating the checks into two stacks.

"Find something?" I asked.

"Maybe."

The two women and I leaned closer. Scott pushed one stack to his left. "Those are ordinary checks." Then he held out four checks in a fan. "These are all made out to Dr. Hiram Kramer, all for seventy-five dollars, each a week apart."

Harriet and Mildred didn't have a clue as to who Hiram was. I had a guess. Maybe a medical doctor, but probably some kind of therapist. We checked the local phone book but found no listing. We tried directory assistance. Hiram had an office in the Loop and lived in Rogers Park on Sheridan Road. We decided against a call and voted for a visit.

We thanked Harriet and Mildred. It was a slender thread, but better than anything else we had to go on.

Scott hurried out to his Porche and came back with enough baseballs for all their nephews and nieces. He gets so many requests for signed baseballs, he started carrying a supply in the car. They beamed at us. They wanted to give us supper, but we managed to beg off.

We drove to the city up I–57 to the Dan Ryan Expressway. Took the Stevenson to Lake Shore Drive and up to where it ends at Hollywood and turned right onto Sheridan. I hit a huge pothole at full speed.

"Easy," Scott said. "We're not even sure he'll be there, or if he'll tell us anything. We probably should have called ahead."

I slowed down, but not much. Hiram Kramer lived in the last high rise before Sheridan Road turns to go around Mundelein College and Loyola University.

He was home. When the security guard mentioned Father Sebastian's name into the phone, the person on the other end gave him permission to let us in. I knew immediately as soon as he opened the door that this was the mysterious stranger who met Sebastian on Sunday nights at Roscoe's: short, slight, with dark hair and a pipe.

He showed us into a living room furnished in books. Eight-foot-high bookcases filled every available wall. A rolltop desk placed in front of one of the floor-to-ceiling windows gaped open. Kramer sat on a swivel chair in front of the desk. He seated us in two canvas-backed captain's chairs, the only other seats in the room except for a long black leather couch.

After our introduction he acknowledged Scott with congratulations on his ninth twenty-game season last year.

Then Kramer settled himself into his chair, leaned back, and placed his stocking-clad feet on an open desk drawer. I explained why we'd come, where we found out about him, and how we needed his help.

He fiddled with his pipe, tamped down the tobacco, then used a lighter. The resulting flame reached at least nine inches on each puff. He grinned in satisfaction and faced us. He needed a beard on his face for the right cliché effect. Instead he showed us yellowed teeth and said, "Even though he's dead, I'm not at liberty to talk about him."

"Someone killed him," I said.

He took the pipe by the bowl and stared at us. "There's been no mention of that in the papers. Why hasn't anyone heard? I can't believe it. His death was shock enough. He was the only good priest I ever knew."

I spoke as persuasively as I knew how, trying to get him to open up. He wouldn't budge. He talked about professional ethics.

"At least tell us about your relationship with Father Sebastian. It had to be more than professional," I said.

He puffed on his pipe thoughtfully for a minute, then said, "I can go into that a little bit. We met in seminary." Both just out of high school, the two of them had discovered a shared interest in medieval chant. Their mutual sexual orientation had led to little more than a bout or two of mechanical fumbling. "We never even got all our clothes off. We decided our friendship was more important than sex. Besides, in those days it was necessary to be exceptionally discreet."

I asked about a liaison with John Smith. I got a surprised look. "How'd you find out about that?"

I told him we'd had a talk with Smith.

He fumbled with his pipe, knocked out the ashes, rearranged some papers on his desk, and finally picked up a pen and tapped one end against the desk. With a conscious effort he stopped fidgeting and gave me a direct look.

"Even if it was murder, what would a thirty-year-old relationship have to do with it?"

"We were hoping you could tell us."

He frowned. "I guess I can tell the story, but it reflects more on me than on Sebastian or Smith." He took a deep breath and began to talk.

Thirty years ago he and Sebastian had been as inseparable as the restrictive rules at the time permitted. Then Smith had entered the picture. For a while the three palled around together. After a while he realized the other two had begun to leave him out of their activities. He'd confronted Sebastian. They'd argued.

He got a soft look in his eyes. They glistened with moisture. "My jealousy consumed me. He offered friendship. I wanted him exclusively. He was so damn kind and understanding. I left the seminary rather than see the two of them together."

Hiram told us he'd done a lot of growing up, got some therapy, and joined a program to become a psychotherapist. During that time Sebastian looked him up. They'd kept in contact. Then two years ago Sebastian had come to him to ask formally to be in therapy. He'd insisted on paying like any other client.

"Were Smith and Sebastian lovers?"

"You mean did they have genital contact?" His eyes flashed angrily. "I have no idea. I didn't want to know then or now. If you mean, were they in love? In a schoolboy-crush way, I suppose you could say yes." His tone and manner, though, said yes, he did care. I thought to myself, some hurts never go away.

Kramer insisted that, while they were still friends, their relationship for the past two years was definitely client and therapist.

"Did he tell you he tested positive for the AIDS antibodies?" I asked.

"That's something I'm not at liberty to discuss."

I sighed. It was impossible to find out anything they'd discussed in therapy. I asked, "Why meet at Roscoe's?"

"Why not? It was convenient. I drove down. It made less of a trek home for him."

"You won't tell us anything?" I asked.

He relit his pipe, then gazed at us over the smoking bowl. "You gentlemen ask for a great deal. I understand your emotional involvement because of your nephew. You aren't the police. I told you all there is about Sebastian and me, but you're a couple of amateurs who can be of little benefit to my former client. It is his interest I need to protect even though he's dead." Puffs of smoke escaped languidly from behind the hand that engulfed the bowl of the pipe. A minute later he put the pipe down and said, "You're obviously used to people being charmed by Mr. Carpenter's fame or perhaps the people you request information from are swept away by the force of your obvious emotion. I'm not. Come back with a court order or put me on the stand. Then I might talk."

Minutes later we gave it up as futile. At Scott's place I called Neil. I told him I wanted the remaining members of the Faith Board of Directors in the penthouse within the hour. He began a few protests, but I issued orders, and for once the old queen shut up and did as he was told.

Five minutes later the intercom phone rang. That was quick, I thought. But it wasn't Faith. The doorman asked us if we'd see Detective Turner.

9

In the living room, Turner inspected Scott's World Series MVP trophies and Cy Young awards. He nodded appreciatively. "I played baseball in high school," he said. He smiled as he took a seat on the couch. "I pitched, but not in your class."

"Why'd you give it up?" Scott asked.

"I went for one of those mass tryouts the White Sox had one summer. Instead of being the star from my team, I was one of four hundred who thought his fastball could strike out the side. It couldn't." He smiled ruefully. "So I became a cop. I like it."

He settled himself on the white leather couch and said, "You boys have been pretty active."

"Wouldn't you be if one of your family'd been kidnapped?" I said.

He held up a hand. "I'm not criticizing. Not yet, anyway. I will tell you this. While there is no longer overt opposition to a murder investigation, I've never felt such pressure from the higher-ups to go easy. That's one thing. But the pressure also comes in weird indirect ways too. It's like being beaten to death with an all-day sucker. Reports that usually take an hour take a day. If they used to take a day, they take a week. Only somebody with powerful clout could pull those kinds of strings. Every little bureaucratic inconvenience somebody can put in my way in investigating this has been there. Plus I keep hearing about you guys. Your friend Prentice complained to the beat cop. Our guy wasn't too sympathetic. Prentice had no witnesses and wasn't willing to show any bruises from the torture."

Scott said, "I tried to twist his dick and balls off."

Turner said, "You've got to let the cops handle this."

"They haven't solved it," I snapped.

"Neither have you," he countered. "What you *have* done is piss people off or scare them away. I admit I wouldn't be pursuing this, at some danger to my career I might add, if I didn't believe you. However, I'm not going to risk my job for a couple of fuck-ups. I'm not going to tell you to stop. I know you won't. This is a warning. If you're caught in anything even slightly illegal, you're dead meat. Besides shit from me and the rest of the police department, whoever's behind the cover-up—and we all suspect the Church—has more power than even the most popular baseball player."

"They'd hurt us?"

"Oh, yes, but in subtle ways. It'd be as if they were slicing off your skin layer by layer. Painful torture and eventual death. They won't call a press conference to denounce you. I've seen the Church do this kind of thing before. Somebody will be a friend of the owner of the team, and with a whisper in his ear, suddenly you find yourself traded away. That's one small example of a thousand kinds of revenge they might take. Be careful. Go easy."

We thanked him for the warning.

"I'm also here to tell you that Father Sebastian was poisoned."

We gaped in astonishment.

"The Catholic Church isn't the only institution around here with hidden powers." He said that, like the HIV test, other parts of the autopsy had been done before official word came down to cool it. "My source wasn't able to find out what kind of poison," he said. They planned further tests. For now, they were questioning all the people at the rectory who might have had access to his food.

I couldn't see Mildred and Harriet Weber as murderers.

We told him all we knew. He left around eight-thirty, after a final warning.

The members of the Faith Board of Directors arrived within fifteen minutes of one another, a half hour after Turner left.

Neil came first. He permitted himself a detailed inspection of the decor in the living room and kitchen. We didn't take him on a tour.

"How butch," he murmured, descending the steps to the fireplace alcove. "All it needs is a white bearskin rug, and I'd orgasm as I stand here."

"Please don't," I muttered.

"And I love the paintings. Who did you get to do them?"

"A friend," Scott said.

Neil swished over to inspect the signatures. "Never heard of him," he said, peering at the painting.

"He's probably never heard of you," Scott said.

Neil harrumphed. He came back to the center of the fireplace area. "What did you boys do to Prentice? To get him over here, I had to threaten the child within an inch of his life." He pointed to Scott. "He especially doesn't like you."

"It's mutual," Scott said.

The buzz of the lobby phone interrupted any further rejoinders. Clayton, whom we hadn't seen since we interviewed him in Bruce's Halfway There bar, entered, followed soon after by Prentice and Monica, arriving at the same time.

When I'd seated them around the fireplace and we'd gotten them drinks, I explained the situation to them. I concluded, "Bartholomew is dead, Sebastian murdered, my nephew missing. I think one person or group is responsible." I paced the room as I spoke. They sat on the matching white leather sofas, Prentice farthest from Scott.

"Has anybody heard from Priscilla?" I asked.

Universal head shakes. I sat on the arm of the couch next to Prentice. He looked up at me, then away. "Where could they hide a kid?" I asked. "This isn't Beirut."

"Maybe they went underground like radicals from the sixties," Clayton suggested.

"Does that still happen?" Neil asked.

"People can and do," Monica said. "It's easier than you think." She explained that without her knowledge the Lesbians for Freedom and Dignity had hidden away for months in the church complex renovation. "You need a group small enough, and people who know how to keep their mouths shut." She shrugged. "It's obviously happening in this instance." She picked up her purse from the floor, drew a gold cigarette case and holder out, looked around the room. "Does anyone mind?"

Scott found her an ashtray while she lit up and struck an elegant pose.

Neil rose, twirled, and flounced to the window. I never found his aging Queen Mother act less amusing. "It's useless for us to pursue this." He returned to stand above us. "We shouldn't have gotten you involved."

"We only did because of Jerry," Scott said. "I don't give a shit about your lesbians, your causes, your goddam religion, your goddam priests, or your petty quarrels. I'm not sure I care that Sebastian is dead. Although out of this whole group, he seems to be the only genuinely good person. Bartholomew died and I feel sorry for him."

"The deaths have to be connected," I said.

Prentice said, "Why are we here?"

"Because we need help," I said. "The Church has shut us out. The cops don't want us to interfere. The only chance left is the lesbian connection. You knew some of these people. All of you at least knew Priscilla. Where would she go?"

Clayton said, "The police asked us the same thing. We've already told them all we know."

"Which is nothing," Monica said. She twirled her hand and cigarette.

We urged them to try again. To think of anything that they hadn't thought of when the police questioned them. I turned to

Clayton. "I haven't had the chance to ask you. Did you know Sebastian was HIV positive?"

He gave me a puzzled look. "No. I don't believe it. He always defended priests' being celibate."

I assured him it was true. I went back to urging them to try and think of anything that might help.

Monica reported that the police search of Priscilla's apartment had led to nothing.

"Can we see her place?" I asked.

A momentary look of annoyance crossed her face. Then she gave a cold smile and said of course we could.

We talked for another half hour, trying various remembrances. Prentice claimed he knew very little about his sister's life. I confronted him with the fact that he knew of their secret hiding place. His response was that as far as he knew the place wasn't a secret. He never knew any of their last names or anything of their backgrounds. "They didn't plot revolution while I was around," he claimed.

Scott, Monica, and I shared a cab to the *Gay Tribune* offices. Night breezes stirred the air as we rode over. Instead of the usual clearing after a winter storm, it'd turned close and clammy. As we drove we could see the tops of the taller Loop buildings obscured by low-hanging clouds that had moved in with the sunset. The weatherman on the cab's radio said we were between two jet streams. If one moved north, it would probably snow. If the other moved south, it would turn bitter cold.

Priscilla's apartment proved to be as spartan as she herself was. She had basically two rooms plus a minuscule bath. The bedroom contained a twin bed that had a bright red-checked bedspread. The bed, a simple chair, and barren nightstand were the only furniture. A two-foot-by-two-foot charcoal sketch of a nude woman seen from the side hung on the wall.

The kitchen–living room had a worn old couch and three mismatched faded chairs grouped to face the kitchen table. There was a two-burner stove and a half refrigerator. A door next to the refrigerator led to a tiny washroom. A person could barely turn around in the shower space. We stood in the kitchen area talking.

"What does she do for money?" I asked.

Monica said, "I don't know about her personal finances. She never goes out to eat." She pointed to the row of health food cereal boxes. "She eats here or not at all. A couple of the others used to tease her that she subsisted on gruel." She smiled bleakly. "Priscilla cares about causes and not much else," she said.

"I'm not sure I disagree about the causes, just the methods," I said. I inspected kitchen cupboards and drawers as we spoke. I found three or four soup spoons, a few forks, three plastic dishes, a cereal bowl, one pot, and one pan. "What's she doing for money?" I reasked.

"As I said, she never spends for food beyond the basics. She buys inexpensive clothes. Her salary from the paper isn't great, but she could've afforded more than this. She may have stashed away a great deal. The police didn't find any bankbooks or shoe boxes stuffed with money when they searched." Stuffing money in shoe boxes is an old Illinois political tradition.

The phone rang. We stared at it and then at each other.

Monica glided to the receiver and picked it up. Her hello sounded sultry enough to put half a dozen madams out of business. She listened a moment, then said, "You're sure?" and waited. She replaced the receiver. "Clayton. He's seen Priscilla."

Clayton had gotten off the el at the Loyola stop. He lived in the building next to the el tracks. In the alley between he'd seen Priscilla.

"He said he'd follow her as best he could and call us as soon as she stopped somewhere," Monica said.

"Where could she be headed?" I asked.

Monica shrugged. "I have no idea."

We settled in the *Gay Tribune* offices one floor down and waited for a call from Clayton. Monica sat at a desk, her feet up, smoking cigarettes. Scott sat on a couch in an open waiting area, leafing through back issues of the paper. I paced the room, willing the light on the phone to begin flicking.

Monica spent some of the time filling us in on Prentice and Priscilla. They were actually half-brother and -sister. Their mother remarried when Priscilla was eight. They'd grown up in Oak Park in a pleasantly upper-middle-class home. With mother and dad working, Priscilla often found herself caring for her little brother. From age twelve to sixteen her social life revolved around her parents' schedule of evening meetings. Instead of resenting the kid, she'd grown quite fond of him. She told Monica the only one she missed on leaving home for college was Prentice. Brother and sister had a falling out about his hustling but had achieved a reconciliation sufficient to the point that they made a joint coming-out presentation to their mother. This had been three years ago. It had gone badly. Monica wasn't sure if they'd spoken to the mother since.

The three of us talked about parents and coming out. Two days from now, Scott's mom and dad were due.

At periodic intervals we tried calling Clayton's home. I soon began to dread the opening words of his phone message. At midnight we started phoning hospitals. The newspaper had five outside lines. We each took a separate area directory and began dialing. This left open lines for him to get through on. I had just opened the second directory, which was for the western suburbs, when the phone rang. Monica and Scott were in the middle of calls. I jammed down the flashing button.

Clayton sounded terrifically out of breath.

"Where are you?" I demanded.

"The Wilmette el station. The end of the line."

"She's there?"

"I lost her."

She'd led him a merry chase. They'd ridden the el from Evanston to the Loop, transferred to go down to 95th Street to the end of the line on the south side, then back again. He'd kept her in sight and a car behind, but he thought she'd spotted him the last time they'd transferred. She'd been talking to a woman he didn't recognize on the el platform. Usually he'd had to wait and make a mad dash just before the doors of the train closed so she wouldn't notice him on the platform. All he'd heard was she was meeting Prentice. She'd gotten off at the Willmette end of the line and stepped into a cab. He hadn't gotten the number of the vehicle.

I hung up and told the others. I finished, "That shit Prentice knew all along." We got his home number from directory assistance. No answer. We tried Bruce's. He wasn't on duty. I knew he worked for Neil at times. I tried calling him. I slammed the phone down on Neil's supercilious message. If Prentice had a trick, Neil might know where he'd take him. Monica decided she'd sleep in Priscilla's apartment instead of going home. She could catch any calls that might come in.

Outside, the mist had changed to a light snow with occasional gusts of wind.

"Following Prentice and torturing him for answers based on a slightly overheard conversation isn't much," Scott said as we walked up Halsted toward Fullerton.

"I'm sure that little bastard's the key," I said. "I'm surprised you're not eager to track him down."

"I've been hit in the nuts with a line drive. I know what kind of pain I inflicted on him. He told all he knew."

I still wanted to check with Neil. The best place to find him was among the reigning queens of Chicago gaydom who held court nightly at the Melrose Restaurant from one until until three or four in the morning.

We found Neil just settling in. He grumbled when we told him we needed to talk. He excused himself and lumbered onto the sidewalk. The snow was deep enough now to show outlines of footprints.

"I want Prentice. Now. Where is he?"

"He only works for me part time. He doesn't check in every instant."

"Where is he?" I demanded.

"With a trick, I suppose. I have no idea where."

"Is he with a rich businessman in a fancy hotel or in a fancy suburban mansion or at an after-hours club?"

"I can't have my clients disturbed," Neil said.

"You can have your face rubbed in fresh snow," Scott said.

Neil drew himself up to his full fairyed fury height. "Listen, you ignorant hick!"

"Neil, please. Remember my nephew. We promise not to bother them. We'll wait until he's done. I promise."

"I got you into this." He shook his head. "I don't think he knows anything. I asked him myself. He told me he knew nothing." I felt flakes of snow melting on my forehead and forming minor rivulets down my cheeks. I swiped at them with a gloved hand. I repeated my plea.

Neil sighed. "Try the Conrad Hilton. It shouldn't be an all-nighter. You're probably too late as it is."

We raced off. We found a cab and took it to Scott's. There we transferred to my truck. With the gathering snow I wanted four-wheel drive and not cabdrivers to rely on. We took Michigan Avenue. The few cars on the deserted streets swayed and swerved in the deepening snow. We saw no plows or salt trucks. With oversized tires and four-wheel drive, my truck purred through the streets easily.

Neil wouldn't give us the client's name. He said it wouldn't make any difference. The guy would be registered under a fake one.

We parked on Michigan Avenue in such a way that we could see the side and front entrances. I kept the motor running. I put the wipers on intermittent and left the defroster on. We waited less than ten minutes. Neil was right. Prentice had been almost through. The kid sauntered out the front door, leather jacket open. One of the doormen tried to flag down a cab. I thought of driving up and trying to grab him, but didn't like the prospects with so many witnesses around.

It took longer for us to wait for him to get a cab than it did for him to come out. Besides the fact that it was late, the weather kept every cab busy. Finally one pulled up to disgorge passengers. Prentice hopped in after dropping a tip into the doorman's hand.

We followed the cab. They swung out Balbo to Lake Shore Drive, then turned north. At first I feared he might simply be going home. When we passed the Fullerton exit I breathed easier. I knew he lived near Fullerton and Clark. If he was going home, they'd have exited there. We swept north into a gathering wind which now slanted in from the northeast off Lake Michigan. We could see waves crashing on the beaches. In Chicago a northeast wind in winter often means a rising storm and possibly tons of snow. It had been sixty-three degrees the day before the great storm of 1967 dropped twenty-three inches of snow on the city.

The slow going had even the light traffic moving at a crawl. Following was easy. At the end of the Drive they turned north on Sheridan Road. Minutes later the cab stopped under the Loyola Avenue el tracks. I hoped we weren't in for a protracted chase around the city on the el. Prentice eased out of the cab, crossed the street, and walked northwest next to the el wall. Several cars behind us beeped as we waited for the traffic to clear. I didn't want to pass or lose Prentice. I pulled into the parking lot for the first apartment house on the south side of the street. Numerous signs warned of towing and fines for illegal parking. I ignored them. We had more important problems. Besides, with the storm, tow trucks would be busy removing cars from snow routes, I hoped. The last thing we heard before turning the truck off was the weather forecast predicting six inches or more of snow.

From the cab of the truck we watched Prentice enter the alley that ran along the concrete barrier of the el tracks. We hurried out of the truck and ran to the shadows of the building on the north side of the street. The wind and snow stung my face as I peered around the corner. Prentice trudged on, keeping to the far side of the alley near the el wall, which afforded some relief from the wind.

We slipped from shadow to shadow behind him. He glanced

around occasionally but most often kept his head hunched between his shoulders in his leather jacket. For three blocks we followed the alley. The damn thing was far too well lit. What I wouldn't have given for a dark, threatening urban alley with scurrying rats! Several times we had to wait until he rounded a curve before we could move. At Morse Avenue he turned west. With the wind behind him, he moved more quickly. We encountered few pedestrians, but of these a few eyed us suspiciously as we waited in doorways.

Up the hill to Clark Street and then north again. Cars swished slowly by. Snow scrunched under our feet. The steps of those who had passed before us filled rapidly with falling snow.

A half block past Morse, the street offered no more hiding places, and we had to stay hidden longer than usual. We watched Prentice cross Lunt Street at the light. He began to turn to look back and we pushed farther into the doorway. When we looked out, he was gone. No cars passed at the moment so he hadn't jumped into one. Both sides of the street were empty of pedestrians.

We hurried forward. At the intersection I began a dash across, but Scott grabbed me as a car I hadn't noticed scrunched toward us from the west.

"Thanks," I said. "Was he in that car?"

"Only if he had the time to slip into seventy-year-old grandmother drag."

A few brave souls hurried along the sidewalks. None of them looked remotely like Prentice. We hurried back to Lunt Street and checked it for a half a block in either direction. No luck. On our way back to Clark Street I even opened the top of a dark green dumpster. Empty of garbage and Prentice. We raced carefully up and down both sides of Clark Street, gradually becoming less cautious, staring in the windows of silent businesses as we realized we might have lost him.

We returned to the intersection where he had disappeared. We sheltered on the northwest corner of the street under the overhang of a deserted savings and loan building. It'd gone belly up a few years before. A larger concern bought them out and moved the operation a block north to a modern facility. They hadn't been able to rent the place since.

"Where'd he go?" Scott said.

"Here," I said jerking a thumb at the looming gray mass behind us.

Scott looked at me.

"He couldn't have gone down the streets or we'd have seen him. We looked in the businesses. Every storefront is occupied and looks legitimate. He couldn't have reached the next cross street. We weren't that far behind. It's the only deserted place around."

"We're not breaking into this one unless we're absolutely sure. Remember what Turner said. No lawbreaking. I'll go along if, for sure, somebody's in here."

I agreed. We made a slow, careful search around the perimeter.

"Look." Scott pointed to the ground.

I observed two sets of rapidly filing footprints behind us. "That's us. So?" It dawned on me. Ours were the only prints around the back and side of building. The two sidewalks in front had enough smeared footprints that figuring out which were Prentice's was impossible.

"The place is shut tight. He's not in there," Scott said disgustedly.

A few doors down on Clark Street, across from the Dunkin Donuts, sat a small diner from which I thought we could observe any activity in the bank building. From the pay phone in front I called the Twenty-third District to talk to Turner. He told us not to bother Prentice. He might be a suspect, but he wasn't guilty of anything yet. After listening to a final warning to leave him alone, I hung up. I joined Scott at a booth next to the front windows. The panes had several layers of encrusted grease and dirt on them. I tried making a hole in the grime-covered pane. After using six napkins from the holder on the table, I got a streaky view of the driving storm and the black mass of the three-story bank building.

"They're in there. I know it," I said.

"What'd he do, fly in?"

I realize Scott is gorgeous, wonderful, tall, handsome, fabulously rich, and very sexy, but at times he's annoying as hell. This was one of those times. I made the only rational response to his sarcasm. I stuck my tongue out at him.

The waiter, a dwarf, arrived to see this example of modern open communication. He noticed the gap I made in the window.

"Storm's getting worse." He spoke in a refined British accent. "What can I get you gentlemen?"

I ordered coffee and a burger. The dwarf turned to Scott. "And for you, Mr. Carpenter?" We got the autograph and handshakes out of the way. As he waddled off to place our order, I took a more careful look around. The only other customer was a guy in a trenchcoat slumped over some coffee at the counter. In good weather he looked like he'd be the neighborhood flasher. The dwarf didn't reappear, but I heard banging and clattering in the kitchen.

Minutes later he showed up with surprisingly good food. He noticed me peering out the window. I'd had to clear it several more times.

He pointed to the pile of napkins. "Something wrong?" he asked.

I nodded my head across at the bank. "You know anything about that place?"

"Closed a year ago. Had my savings there. Good thing it was insured. They indicted the former president last week." He snorted contemptuously. "He defrauded the place of tens of millions. He'll get fined a little, do a short term in jail, and live like a king for the rest of his life. I'd like a try at that."

"I mean more recently. People hanging around. Lights that shouldn't be on."

He moved closer to the table. He stared at me. "You a cop?"

I admitted I wasn't.

"What's your interest?"

I explained briefly. He nodded several times. He turned and brought a chair over, which he clambered onto. We saw him at eye level. He wore a dirty apron over white pants and a T-shirt. He wiped his hands on a towel he had hooked in his belt. His shrewd blue eyes examined each of us in turn.

"This is a closed-mouth neighborhood," he said. "People mind their own business. We've got a cosmopolitan mix here. People get sensitive very quickly. We leave each other alone. I have my little kingdom here and live upstairs." The other customer got up and staggered to the cash register. With deft movements he climbed down, strode to the register, took the man's money, and returned.

He told us his name was Fred Brown. We listened to a great deal of his family history, which included an uncle who was one of the Munchkins in the *Wizard of Oz*. In three years he planned to retire and move to some low-tax island in the Caribbean. It took forever, but he finally got back to the topic of the bank. He leaned closer, spreading his hands flat on the tabletop. "Something is screwy over there. Once or twice I thought I saw lights around two, after I closed up here. I almost called the cops once, but . . ." He shook his head. "I thought it was a trick of the streetlights." He shrugged. "I even went over one morning about nine. The place is nailed shut from top to bottom and all around." He'd noticed a couple of pleasant young women new in the neighborhood. He didn't get many customers besides his regulars. Most people didn't like the looks of his restaurant from the outside. We described the women from the other night, especially Priscilla and Stephanie. He didn't remember seeing them.

We took a last walk around the deserted bank. We saw only faint traces of our own footsteps in back and in the alley. On the side street the jumble of footprints had almost disappeared. When we got back to the corner of Clark and Lunt, Scott said, "Let's go home. It's going to be a hell of a storm. We lost him. We'll find him again."

I sighed. "Yeah." We crossed the street to begin the trudge back to the truck. Nearly three now, we saw neither traffic nor pedestrians. I thought about the forlorn hope of hailing a cab as I turned to give one last look back at the bank. Doing so, I almost crashed into an overturned trash can. I managed to twist my ankle, avoiding the pile of leftover debris.

"That's it!" I shouted. "The dumpster!"

"What?" Scott sounded annoyed. "He's not hiding in an overgrown trash can. You looked, remember."

"That's how he got in. It's next to the sidewalk on the street side, so all the tracks on the sidewalk would be mushed together. Fred wouldn't notice it. It's too far back. You can't see the dumpster from the restaurant."

We hurried back to the bank. We examined the snow on the lid.

"It's been snowing hard for a while," I said. "I don't remember for sure, but when we got here before, I think there was only a thin film of snow on the dumpster, and you can get up on the top of this thing without stepping into the alley. Somebody brushed away the snow and tracks from one of those windows." I pointed to the openings on the second floor.

Scott looked doubtful. I scrambled onto the dumpster. It creaked rustily but stayed in place. Two windows offered possible entrances. Carefully I inched to the nearest one on my right. I didn't want to show myself to someone inside. The second-floor opening revealed little. Someone had driven nails into all the sides of the window pane. I inched to the left. I did not shout with joy, but I beckoned Scott up. We teetered together on the lid. I glanced at the 3 A.M. street. Nothing disturbed the fallen snow. I pointed toward the window. Little mounds of disturbed snow lay heaped on the sill. I rubbed the sides with a gloved hand. I had to lean close to see. The absence of nails was suggestive, recent skid marks conclusive. There was no doubt the window had been used recently.

"We're going in," I said.

I got a litany of nasty possibilities from Scott, including too dangerous, call the cops, breaking the law.

"We can't stand here like this arguing," I said. "Remember the other night? By the time the cops get here and maybe get a warrant, the women could be gone again. And Jerry might be here."

I watched bits of snow land in his hair and on his face. His deep voice rumbled several more objections before he finally gave a grudging okay.

I reinspected the window. No light shone from within. If it was an entrance, I doubted if anybody slept in such a room. If they'd posted a guard we were in deep shit. For a few seconds I thought about Sally Holroyd, the woman Monica had mentioned who had terrorist training. I didn't want to try my rusty fighting skills against her youthful madness.

The window rose with surprising ease and silence. They'd oiled it. The opening was approximately two feet by four. An old-fashioned window from when they'd built the place seventy years ago, wide enough for the gargantuan woman of the other night. I eased inside. Scott followed quickly. He shut the window. I waited for my eyes to adjust to the darkness. The window let in enough light so I could see we were in a former bathroom. Cracked urinals on the left side told me it was a men's room. Someone had ripped out the dividers between the stalls on the right. The lidless toilets gaped at us. I listened intently. I heard Scott's breathing and the rustle of his jacket. The muffled swish of a car's tires passing outside penetrated into the darkness. Nothing from inside the building.

The place smelled musty and even felt somewhat comfortable after the storm and cold outdoors. The beaded glass in the door didn't let in any light from inside the building. We eased across the floor. The cold doorknob turned with an unpleasantly loud creak, but the door itself moved noiselessly as I pulled it forward inch by inch. Dark eddies and swirls lurked in the unlighted corridor. An occasional lighter grayness, remnants of beams of distant streetlights, softened the shadows in a corner or two. I let my eyes adjust to the dimness. I listened carefully. Not a sound.

Because of the slope of the hill back from Clark Street, the rear of the building had four floors visible from the alley in back but only three in front, plus a small tower nestled one story up in the back. I didn't know if there were basements and sub-basements to explore. Plus we were inside illegally with no guarantee that a renegade terrorist with a lethal weapon didn't wait at the end of our quest. Fortunately, the possibility of a sleepless neighbor calling the cops was remote. On this side of the street after the bank came the alley, then the Northwestern railroad tracks, two stories high. Across the street, shuttered businesses offered no threat. At 3 A.M. the deserted snow-encrusted streets offered a grim protection.

Finally fully in the doorway, I tried to get my bearings. To the left, a lengthy corridor stretched past shut and silent doors. The darkness made the end indiscernable. To the right, next to an elevator, a narrow staircase led up.

"They were on the top floor last time." I felt Scott's lips brush my ear as he whispered and then pointed toward the stairs.

It was as good a guess as any. The building wasn't as complex as the last one, but I presumed it had its eccentricities. I didn't want a repeat of last time.

Up we climbed. Each creak of the damn stairs froze us into tense moments of listening. My eyes rose above the level of the next floor while still climbing. I carefully scanned the lengthy corridor. It matched the one below: airless and dank with no sign of human habitation. We turned and climbed the next flight of stairs. I peered to the right. Here the elevator shaft had no doors. The opening gaped into nothingness. On the other side of this empty space, the hall turned abruptly to the right. I inched to the opening. Greater darkness than that which we were now in filled the shaft. For an instant I wondered why my fabled jungle training hadn't included the simple idea of going to an Osco Drug Store to buy a cheap flashlight.

Listening at the edge of the blackness, I thought I heard several muffled bangs and perhaps a murmur of laughter. I couldn't tell if the noise came from above, from below, or was maybe just a trick my overstrained senses played on me.

150

The stairs we had ascended ended on this floor. The long corridor to the left offered no nooks and crannies to hide behind. I pointed to the right. Scott nodded. I eased to the other side of the hall. I thought I heard a foot shuffle ahead and reached back my hand to halt Scott, but he was closer than I thought. We bumped. He stumbled. For a second he teetered toward the four-story fall. I grabbed him back. He hit the wall with a resounding thump. For several eternities neither of us moved. I strained every sense for a hint of human habitation, rushing pursuit; even the sound of a scurrying rat at this point might ease the tension. Total silence.

Retreat was pointless. We pushed on. The corridor now twisted through several turns. Each time I listened before looking around the next bend.

After the second turn we found a janitor's closet. Propped on the floor, no longer connected to any pipes, was a washbasin deep enough for buckets to be filled in. A string mop with three remaining strands kept the sink company.

Along one of the corridors, one of the doors had had the beaded glass smashed out of it. We looked through and saw an empty room. Farther on, after a third turn, we came to a doorless room. It had no floor for several feet just inside the doorway. If we'd entered unknowingly, we could have dropped painfully far. I tried to see down, but no light escaped from below. Against the walls stood scaffolding on which sat several paint cans. I detected no scent of paint old or new. Somebody may have started a rehab and never finished.

Two more turns and the corridor dead-ended at a massive door. This had to be the entrance to the small fifth-floor tower we'd seen from outside. I felt along the edges. In the darkness I touched the knob and tried a gentle twist. It wouldn't move. I continued my explorations by feel. I discovered hinges along the left side. The door opened inward. I tried yanking at the pins with my gloved hand. I couldn't get any kind of grip. I took off my gloves, to try and pry better. In frustration I pulled too hard. The pin popped out and clattered to the floor while managing to open a gash in my hand.

Still I listened for any sounds of approaching humans. Was that the old building creaking distantly or a stealthy footstep inches away from the last corner a couple yards behind us? There was no possible escape if the troops came up behind. We had to go forward. In frustrated silence I pulled, tugged, yanked, twisted, and grabbed at the pin of the second hinge. The sweat on my hands prevented any kind of grip. I moved so Scott could give it a try. I sucked at the blood seeping from my wound. After a minute the pin rasped softly into the palm of his hand. He crouched to reach for the third hinge. Did I finally hear a rat patter nearby or was it a slithering footstep meant to be silent? Ears playing tricks or not, I wanted out of this building.

Scott couldn't budge the last pin. I tried again. No luck. He worked at it again, swearing continuously under his breath.

"Let's go," I whispered.

"We're in. We're finding what we need to know before we go." He stood up. "Hold the door up by the handle." I obeyed the barely audible command. The door was loose, and I could hear the metal click in the two empty hinges. Scott put his shoulder to the door and shoved hard. With a sharp crack and clang the pin broke, the knob popped out of my hand, and the door fell. The sound echoed horribly.

"Fuck," I said.

He concentrated on moving the door aside. Quickly I joined him. Finished, we returned to see an entryway followed by a short flight of stairs that led up to a modern door with an emergency bar, fortunately on our side. Before I could reach the top of the stairs, the door abruptly swung open from the other side. The gargantuan woman named Stephanie, who'd sensed our presence two nights ago, gaped at us. Her bulk blocked a feeble light that glowed from behind her.

"You!" she bellowed.

I rushed up the last two steps and put my shoulder into her midsection to blast her out of the way. Instead of moving her, I sank into her. She grabbed my arm and flung me into the room: a tactical mistake, with Scott now in front and me behind. In the tiny room by flickering candlelight I saw she wasn't the only one present. A small person with its back to us lay huddled in the corner. From the jacket I knew it was Jerry. I didn't have time to call out or go to him because Stephanie lurched into me. Scott had hold of one arm and half of her torso. She struggled madly with him. We might be in good shape, and he especially strong, but she out weighed the two of us combined by at least a hundred pounds. I managed to grab a leg and a handful of hair. I twisted both. She yelped and let go of Scott and turned her fury on me.

In a larger room I could have outmanuevered her. In the confined space she had the advantage. On the other side of her massiveness I saw Scott go to Jerry.

Groggy and unsteady the boy rose. He took a wobbly step, recognized Scott, and flung himself into his arms. The bulk saw my look and turned to attack them, so I struck. I managed to entangle her feet and over she toppled, missing me by six inches.

I grabbed one of her hands and bent her fingers almost double backwards to immobilize her with pain. She squawked and gasped. I saw her readying a full-throated roar.

I stuffed the corner of a nearby blanket in her gaping maw. Scott whipped his belt off and quickly wrapped it around her ankles. She struggled violently again, but her immobilized legs prevented renewed hostilities. Moments later we had her hands uncomfortably secured to an old radiator.

Panting hard I turned to Jerry. He had a black eye. He threw himself into my arms and I hugged him close.

He said, "I knew you'd get here, Uncle Tom."

With all the noise, I presumed we had scant seconds to flee. Quickly I checked Jerry. Other than being scared, dirty, and cold, he seemed okay. We got the hell out of there. Back the way we came, more careful than ever and more concerned because we knew for sure now that the women were here.

At the elevator shaft there was no doubt about the sounds of humans stirring below. Seconds later, footsteps echoed at the far end of the long corridor.

◣ 10 ◥

They used no lights. For a few seconds I wondered why. I guessed because they still feared detection and couldn't risk random flashings, which might be observable from outside.

I listened at the steps and heard no sound from below. "Jerry, is there another way out?" I asked in a whisper.

"I don't know," he said. "Sorry. Maybe on the ground floor. I was pretty confused when they dragged me up here."

Ominous shadows moved in the darkness down the corridor toward us.

We rushed down the stairs; Scott in the lead, Jerry in the middle, and me bringing up the rear. The darkness kept us from full speed, but our eyes were accustomed enough to the dark to make decent progress. Down a flight of stairs and into the third-floor corridor. Silence reigned in front of us, but there was a thunder of pursuit above us. At the top of the landing we paused for a second: still nothing from the steps below. Down we hurried toward the second floor and the exit.

The darkness and our need for haste produced the disaster that followed. One second I felt steps beneath my feet. Then, from in front, I heard Scott say, "Oh, shit!" along with assorted curses from numerous other voices. I didn't have time to stop or attempt a retreat. I tripped over Jerry and sprawled into a mass of struggling bodies. I couldn't tell how many of them

154

assaulted us. I wasn't even sure which way to punch. Fortunately they were similarly hampered. Random elbows, feet, fists, and fingers probed and gouged. I heard voices calling from just a few feet above us. Reinforcements for them.

"Jerry!" I yelled.

"Here." I heard his voice not more than a foot away on my right.

I groped in the darkness and grabbed his arm.

"Scott!" I yelled and heard only grunts for an answer, my lover's indistinguishable from the others. The troops from above clattered into us. I managed to keep a grip on Jerry, but it limited my ability to fight. I managed to claw my way down and off the stairs. For a second the mass of bodies parted right in front of me.

Walter Payton slicing through an opposing team in his glory days was as nothing compared to the moves I made then. I kept hold of Jerry. Moments later, free of the mingling mob, we raced down the second-floor corridor. For a few seconds they didn't pursue.

"Where are they?" I heard total fury in Priscilla's voice.

I wanted to turn back to make sure Scott was safe. Then I heard his voice, I thought from a distance, perhaps the stairs. "Run!" he yelled. "I'll meet you outside."

"Never!" Priscilla bellowed. And the chase was on. The corridor ended in a right-angle turn. My feet slipped briefly at the sharpness of the turn, but I steadied my hand on the wall. I felt more than saw Jerry next to me. This hall ended in a door with a broken exit sign above it. On the other side of it I tried to find something to jam it shut. No luck. The stairs led down. Hands pulled on the knob, trying to yank it out of my hand. I held tight. Fists began to pound on the door.

"Keep going," I ordered Jerry.

"Where?" he panted. Sometimes I wish he wasn't as independent and stubborn as his uncle. I could barely see his features in the dark, but I caught the glint of his eyes.

I didn't want to hold this position too long. I feared they knew other ways to come up behind us. I turned the knob. Instead of resisting the next furious yank from the other side, I shoved the door inward. I heard curses, yells, and falling bodies. Jerry and I turned and ran.

Down the last flight of stairs we flew. On the ground floor of the old bank, we turned to the main doors. A moment's inspection confirmed the view from outside: solidly boarded up and tightly nailed shut.

Into the main lobby. To the left were the old teller's windows, serrated blocks of fake marble, dust encrusted and empty. To the right occasional mounds of debris were all that remained of where bank officers once sat. Sounds of pursuit came from the front. Desperately we hunted for a rear exit. Finally, in the darkness at the back we faced two gaping doorways. Neither emitted any light. We chose the one on the right. After a short hall, steps abruptly started down. I didn't like this, but we couldn't go back. As we reached the bottom of the stairs a faint glow began to show ahead of us. Outdoor light, I hoped. We rushed past a series of cubicles with frosted glass walls that reached three quarters of the way to the ceiling.

The light grew. "I don't like this," I said. It felt wrong. We had to be in a basement. I couldn't imagine where the glow came from.

We turned a corner. The vault of the old bank gaped at us. The door leaned against the wall on our right, unhinged and crumbling. A prosaic floor lamp gave enough light for us to see sleeping bags, a couple of folding chairs, clothes strewn on the floor, a hot plate piled with a few miniature pots and pans. Bad choice.

The enemy appeared at the opening behind us, Stephanie and Priscilla, walking slowly toward us. Two other women stood in the doorway. I wondered if one of them was the terrorist.

Priscilla began. "Give up—"

I launched myself at Stephanie aiming to push her into the women at the door. "Run!" I yelled to Jerry. In seconds I was in the middle of a flailing mob of bodies. No high school, college, or pro football pile-up could match it for closeness, violence, or pain.

For an instant I managed to get on my feet. I glanced around for Jerry, didn't see him, and took a step to run. Too late. Priscilla grabbed my right leg. I toppled over. Stephanie got a large chunk of her body on top of my chest. I felt searing pain, bellowed, then passed out.

I woke staring up at a light. I hurt all over. I tried to move my left arm. Pain leaped up and down my side. I tried my right arm. I could barely move it, but the pain wasn't as great. Despite the agony I ordered my feet to move. I heard a groan, realized it was me. I managed to bend my legs at the knee and got my feet flat on the floor. I turned my head to the right and saw wall. I tried to the left. Stephanie sat there with a two-by-four in her massive paws. She lowered it to my knee caps and tapped gently against their apex.

"Lower, or I break them," she said.

I eased my knees back down.

"He come around, Stephanie?" I lowered my chin and saw the top third of another woman.

Stephanie grunted a yes.

"If he moves, sit on him. Crush every bone in his fucking body." This woman wore a black warm-up outfit. Lying on the ground, I had a distorted view of her height, but I thought she must be the short woman we followed three nights ago.

"Did they get the other two?" Stephanie asked.

"No. They're gone. We've got to blow this dump in minutes. Priscilla insisted on one last look-through. Stupid. That kind of decision can cost a good unit valuable time and lives."

Less than a minute later, all six women assembled in the little room. Three of them began rapid packing. Their swift work led me to believe they must have had practice drills. Now I knew how they had moved so fast out of their church hideout.

In all the chaos Prentice did not appear. The little shit had escaped again.

Priscilla had come in last. She and the woman in black stood in the doorway arguing. The others ignored them.

"Your goddam brother led them here," the woman said.

Priscilla stabbed a finger at her. "Just like you did at the church, Sally."

"I was protecting you," the other snapped.

Stephanie stood up. Much to my surprise she walked up to the other two, grabbed them each by the back of the neck, and bonked their heads together.

Both women bellowed and tried to assume defensive postures. Stephanie kept her grip. "They can hear this bitch fit all the way from the Loop. You can fight later. Now get your goddam shit together. We're leaving in half a minute." She flung each woman away from her and turned to me. Her bulk looked even more enormous from where I lay. She lumbered over and peered down.

Almost involuntarily I tried to hunch away. I couldn't completely stifle the moan of agony the pain caused.

"Do we bust him some more, kill him, leave him, or what?" Stephanie asked the room at large.

I surveyed the women, all of whom looked at Priscilla.

"Kill him," Sally said.

"Not yet. Bring him along," Priscilla ordered.

Her leadership prevailed. I passed out once during the drag and shuffle as they forced me up to the second floor exit. The shove out the window caused maddening pain, severe enough to keep me from passing out again. Fortunately, I landed on my right side on top of the dumpster. Wildly swirling snow lashed my face as I attempted to rise. The yank from the dumpster into a waiting van was more painful. They tossed me, their sleeping bags, and assorted belongings on the cold metal floor in the back of the van.

I lay gasping for breath, never imagining such pain could exist. I thought playing football in high school and for a year in college had inured me to pain, but this was incredible. Doors slammed. The interior of the van darkened. We began to move.

"Back up the alley, not down," a voice ordered.

"I'm trying," Priscilla said.

I heard the whir of tires stuck in snow. Where were Scott and reinforcements? Maybe he and Jerry were still hidden in the building.

"Rock it back and forth," Sally commanded.

"What the fuck do you think I'm trying to do?" Priscilla snarled.

Seconds of whirring passed. "Get out and push," came the sharp command from in front. Stephanie and the others piled out. Moments later the van began to inch forward. With them preoccupied, I tried boosting myself to my knees. The upward movement and the rocking van caused me to slip. Grasping my left side with my right hand, I barely managed to keep from screaming in agony.

I heard shouts from outside. Doors flew open. They all piled back in. The van slewed left, straightened, and began to move. Stephanie saw me halfway up, gave me a friendly smile, and tapped two fingers against my left side. I cried out and collapsed in pain.

"What's that?" I heard through the haze of pain.

"The macho hero wanted more." Stephanie snickered, then took some rope from around a sleeping bag and tied my hands. From the floor I could make out occasional streetlights. The going seemed extremely slow.

"How deep do you think the snow is?" One of the women in back asked.

"Four inches, maybe more," came an answer.

"It's drifting badly," Stephanie said. "We won't get far. Where are we going?"

Silence as we all strained to hear from the front seats.

"How the fuck should I know?" Priscilla said.

"Good planning, sister." Sally snickered.

A small woman in her fifties, who hadn't spoken before, leaned forward from the third back seat nearest to me. "Where did that kid come from? How come only some of us knew about him? I joined this group for sisterhood, protest, and righteousness, not to cover up somebody's stupid mistakes."

"This whole thing has been one stupid mistake after another," Sally said.

"Then why don't you go back where you came from?" Priscilla said. "We're sick of you and your terrorist-expertise shit. Go back to fucking boys and selling out your womanhood. The only kind of pro you are is the kind that walks the streets."

In a voice that demanded attention Stephanie said, "Where are we going?"

Silence.

She spoke again. "We can worry about political correctness later. Where are we going?"

"The newspaper," was Priscilla's curt reply.

They fought about the advisability of that until the van sideswiped what I guessed was a series of cars. Then silence reigned for several minutes. Listening to the murmur of the tires over snow gave me an odd perspective. Priscilla, our driver, wasn't used to winter weather. She alternately sped ahead, and rode the brakes, slipping and sliding in a variety of directions, often punctuating the more sudden jolts with shouts and curses at opposing drivers. If the snow was continuing to fall at anything like the rate I'd caught a glimpse of, roads that hadn't already begun to close soon would.

Between bouts of pain, I worried about Monica, sleeping at the paper. Would they find her?

For ten minutes of badgering, Priscilla evaded the answer as to why she needed to stop at the newspaper. It took a near mutiny and a particularly violent jolt and swerve for her to say, "Money. We fucking well have to pay for food and gas, don't we?"

This brought silence. My head rocked back and forth in a wide groove on the metal floor. Heat from the surrounding bodies, more than the feeble puffs of warmth coming from the van's heating system, was melting the ice and snow underneath me. The dampness had reached the back of my head and

160

soaked my right pant leg from calf to butt. The snow hadn't filled in Chicago's famed potholes. Each rumble over one caused pain to sear through my chest. As rigid as I tried to hold myself, I couldn't prevent damp, pain, and misery. Any escape was far beyond my capability. I hoped Scott and Jerry had got away in time. Unfortunately, it seemed, so had we.

At the newspaper they engaged in an interminable debate as to who should go inside, who should stay with the van, and what to do with me.

Finally Stephanie said, "For Christ's sake, let's take a vote like we always do and be done with it."

All of them going inside passed five to one. Carrying me along passed four to two. I wished it had lost. They tied a scarf around my entire face to muffle any noise I might try to make. Good thing because, unmuffled, my screams as they jostled me out of the van, and then up the stairs, would have been enough to wake the ghost voters of Chicago. I only passed out once.

Inside, Stephanie propped me between herself and a wall. I didn't have the strength to fight her. I concentrated on breathing easily to keep the pain under control.

A major squabble broke out upstairs. I accidentally began an exasperated breath, which came to a painful halt. There were several loud thumps, as of furniture being rudely tossed aside.

Moments later, two heavily bundled figures hurried toward us down the narrow interior stairs.

"What's up?" Stephanie said.

One of them said, "We quit. They're nuts. We're going back to Boston."

"Stop them!" came a harrowing shriek from the top of the stairs. The two women scuttled out the door.

In the middle of the recriminations, charges, and counter-charges, they let slip the fact that they'd found someone in the building. I feared it was Monica. Moments later, the appearance of the bruised and battered newspaper owner confirmed this. They'd tied her hands. Her open mink coat revealed her evening gown draped in tatters on her body. She glared at her captors but gave me a rueful look and a half smile. They shoved her toward me, telling us both to sit. The push tipped her off balance. She stumbled and landed on top of me. I howled in agony. They ignored us and piled into the composing room, which was on this floor. Stephanie stood in the doorway and ignored us. From the occasional crashes it sounded as if they were breaking every piece of furniture in the place. From what they said, it turned out Priscilla was having trouble finding her hidden stash. She complained that in the cleanup after the last break-in someone had moved her stuff.

Our sarcastic terrorist, who talked in an incongruously high little-girl's whine, voiced mounting contempt and sarcasm at Priscilla's ineptitute.

Meanwhile Monica, realizing my pain, did as much as was possible with her hands tied to ease my discomfort. She asked what happened, but a snarl from Stephanie put a halt to that.

Stephanie did not move to stop what happened next. A deadly silence was broken briefly when Priscilla and Sally exchanged brutal accusations, and then the fight was on. The smashing and crashing of various objects were the only sounds that emanated from the ominously silent foes.

The brief battle ended in a triumphant screech. "Money!" someone yelled. I guessed the tumbling of a piece of furniture had revealed the hiding place.

Stephanie forestalled any renewal of hostilities by a simple suggestion: "Let's go." They almost left without a vote or a debate, but they had to decide what to do with us.

Eventually Monica and I lay together on the floor in back of the van. Priscilla sat in the seat nearest us. Sally took the wheel. In the brief trip from building to van, between bouts of pain, I thought the storm had picked up in intensity. They were in trouble if they thought they could make a daring escape by van. The slipping and sliding on the city streets was worse than before. Priscilla gave directions on getting from Lake Shore Drive to the Stevenson Expressway. I didn't think we hit speeds higher than twenty miles an hour. My perspective only let me see occasional passing street lamps, lighting the wind-driven snow. It hurt too much to raise my arm to see my watch, but it had to be nearly dawn.

I found that if I relaxed my muscles as much as possible while avoiding any movement, the pain was manageable. This was a hell of a trick. I could do it up to seventy-five percent of the time.

"Priscilla, what the hell is going on?" Monica said.

"Tell them to shut the fuck up," said the terrorist from the front.

So Priscilla talked, knowing her rival couldn't leave the wheel to fight. She jerked a thumb at me and said, "Pretty boy here and his jerk lover broke up our last hiding place. I have friends in St. Louis who'll keep us safe and be able to dispose of the prisoners without any trouble."

"Can't we work something out?" Monica asked.

Taking a shot in the dark and speaking between painful gasps, I said, "She and Prentice killed Sebastian. That's why they kidnapped Jerry."

"I don't believe it. What possible reason could they have?" Monica said.

"That gets a little complicated, but I've got the time to explain," Priscilla said. "And since you'll be dead soon anyway, I don't mind telling you."

Monica stared in shock.

Priscilla rubbed her gloved hands together almost gleefully. "It all started when we planned our revolutionary activities," she said. We got a tirade about the male establishment, patriarchal stupidity, and the evilness of the world in general. "Our problem came when we trusted another man." She sighed. "Prentice, as you know, is my brother. He and I were close as children. I felt sorry for him. Plus, he agreed."

"To what?" I asked.

Suddenly the van lurched, swayed, spun. Horns blared and I saw the top of a semi rumble past inches from the windows on the left side of the van. Infighting, recriminations, and finally a resumption of movement followed.

Priscilla said in a stage whisper, "Some people think they know how to lead this group." She pulled her coat closer around herself.

"What did Prentice agree to?" I asked between clenched teeth. The spin had thrown off the rigidly comfortable position I'd managed to achieve.

"Hurts, huh? Good. You managed to fuck everything up. But not as badly as dear naïve Prentice." She sighed. "He agreed to deliver a package to the chancery late at night. We told him it was a harmless smoke bomb. And it would have been, except Sally, our terrorist, isn't as good at making bombs as she claims. Still, we didn't want to kill anyone. If the damn security guard had let the package sit five more minutes, there would have been lots of broken glass, tons of smoke, and maybe a little fire. Unfortunately, he didn't. More unfortunately, Bartholomew got suspicious of Prentice. The old son of a bitch had a date with Prentice that night. Once a month they had sex for half an hour. It's all he could afford after scrimping from his pension each month, and at that Prentice gave him a discount."

She gave a harsh laugh. "Bartholomew had told Prentice he loved him. What a joke. The old fool. Prentice decided to be late for their rendezvous that night. The old bastard went looking for him."

"The old guy was shrewder than you thought," I said. "He suspected something, and he knew where to go."

Priscilla laughed. "Nah. He was lucky. He walked in the front door of Bruce's as Prentice walked out the back. Bartholomew followed, saw the placing of the package—"

"Guessed the contents of the package or the purpose," Monica broke in.

"—and ran for home," Priscilla finished.

Monica said, "He saw the story about the chancery bombing in the paper the next day. I remember how excited he was. Now I know why."

164

"Excited and a blabbermouth. He didn't want to go to the police because he loved Prentice, but he told that goddam Sebastian. Such a fucking goody-two-shoes priest. A saint for our times!" She snorted. "Everybody loved him. Running around listening to people, doing good works."

Another nasty lurch of the van, and pain shot through my side again. They'd crammed their belongings around me tightly, which kept me nearly immobile, an inadvertent kindness that helped keep me from constant agony. My feet were cold. Dampness had crept further into my clothes. As the trip progressed the inside of the windows had fogged up. I was mostly aware of shadows passing. I presumed the lighter shadows represented passing cars, trucks, or streetlights.

Priscilla talked on. Sebastian had gone to Prentice, told him what he knew, urged him to turn himself in. Prentice, not being the brightest, and Sebastian being one of the smartest, figured the prostitute hadn't acted on his own. Prentice blurted out enough of the truth for the priest to guess the Lesbians for Freedom and Dignity were behind it.

Priscilla said, "Sebastian confronted me. I laughed at him. He didn't get mad. He never did. He looked at me with those pitying, priestly, know-it-all eyes and told me if Prentice and I didn't go to the police, he would." She drew a deep breath, rubbed her hand over the window glass, and glanced out the opening she made. "We decided to kill him. Poison in the altar wine. Prentice set up for mass every week so it was easy. That altar wine tastes like shit anyway. We get cases of that generic crap the archdiocese puts out. Sally had connections to some groups that gave us arsenic. We put some in the altar wine."

I'd begun alternately to sweat and shiver. I could no longer distinguish between dampness from the melting snow and sweat from my pain-racked body. I forced my mind to listen to Priscilla's continuing explanation.

On Sundays Prentice had administered the doses Priscilla gave him. She thought it would've acted slower. She shrugged. "I was surprised it took effect so soon. Anyway he died, and we thought we were safe. Then old Bartholomew started up again. The bastard got suspicious. He warned Prentice."

"So he had to die," Monica said.

"Not quite then," Priscilla replied.

Their words came as if from a distance. The pain was all that kept me awake. Each lurch of the van brought me back to full consciousness.

"Of course it was this asshole and his pretty lover who screwed things up." She aimed a kick at me. The sleeping bags and other paraphernalia piled around me spoiled her aim. She missed my ribs, but the jolt to my side was almost as bad. I gasped for air for several minutes.

She explained that our snooping around had worried them. Our relationship with Bartholomew, especially his trust in us, had caused them to take action. They had wanted to avoid killing him, thinking that another death in the group at this time would be too suspicious.

"Him and his buddy"—she jerked a thumb at me—"convinced the old son of a bitch they really cared for him. Bartholomew began to talk about telling them. He got brave enough to threaten Prentice and me together. He had to die."

Prentice had lured him to the trap at Faith headquarters. They started the fire at the front and back downstairs exits.

"I pointed out to most of the members that since we were all conspirators in a murder, whether accidental or deliberate, we'd go to jail just as surely as Prentice. So we decided to grab your nephew to stop you from snooping around." Her tone was ingenuous, almost rueful. "Things got out of hand. Ultimately we didn't know what to do with the kid. We didn't tell the milktoasts in the group, but I couldn't even convince Stephanie to have him killed."

Monica asked, "Why were the *Gay Tribune* offices trashed?"

"Every time you wrote an editorial we disagreed with, the group voted to do it. But you never got the message."

"Why'd Prentice tell us so much about you the first time we talked to him?" I asked.

"He's a blabbermouth who wants to look big and feel important. He thought we were safe. Thinking is not Prentice's strong suit. He figured he'd give you useless information, and you'd go away."

After a jolt from the van and a gasp from me, I managed to ask the next question. "Why'd you threaten Sebastian that Sunday?"

"He talked about going to the police again. I was sick of his shit. I knew he'd be dead soon, and I didn't think I'd be overheard."

She fell silent. I listened to the tires crunching over unplowed snow. I was shivering almost continuously now. I could turn my head just enough to look at Monica. She gave me an encouraging smile mixed with sympathy. As encumbered as I was, although without the pain, she couldn't rescue us.

Priscilla hummed to herself, a toneless sound almost of content and happiness. I dozed between jabs of pain, awakening to cold or heat, shivering and sweating.

The next time I woke clearly, grayness penetrated the misted windows. Full morning. I glanced toward Monica. Her eyes were closed, her mouth slightly open in sleep. My ribs ached, but almost bearably.

"Where are we?" I asked the van at large.

Stephanie's voice sounded sleepy. "Pontiac."

"We're stopped," I said.

"Accident ahead. Must have just happened."

"Go around," Priscilla snapped.

"We should stop to help," Stephanie said.

Priscilla and Sally spoke in unison. "No."

Priscilla said, "We almost hit them because we couldn't see them. Probably nobody can see us from behind either. We've got to get out of here."

I heard the rumble as the driver down-shifted.

"The shoulder's not wide enough," Stephanie said.

"Yes, it is." Sally again.

I felt the van begin to tilt to the right as we inched along the road. The van slipped for a second, tilted more. Someone swore.

"Easy," Stephanie said.

We moved forward, continuing to tilt. I looked over at Monica, now also awake. When disaster came, it took only seconds.

◢ 11 ◣

"Behind us!" someone screamed.

"I'm trying!" came a frantic voice from up front.

The van lurched forward and slid sideways. I heard the tires spinning. One of the horrible sounds of winter is tires refusing to catch hold. Next to the grinding of an engine refusing to start, it's the most depressing sound of the cold.

For an instant I saw a shadow loom behind us and heard the roar of an engine. Then I had a sensation of flying, then falling, and the van tumbled and rolled. The pain in my ribs awakened a thousandfold. I shut my eyes. My tied hands made it impossible to grip anything. Fortunately they'd wedged me among the blankets, clothes, and sleeping bags, which cushioned me from much of the impact. Even so, my tortured ribs caused pain to shoot throughout my body. The van came to rest on its side. Monica and I lay together, half out the now-open back door of the van. We gazed at each other a moment. I felt snow on my check.

"I don't think we're dead," she said. "Are you okay?"

"No," I said.

Both still tied. Trying to keep me from pain as much as possible, Monica managed to inch us the rest of the way out of the van.

Tentatively we stood outside in shin-deep snow gazing at the scene. The storm raged unabated. Snow slanted down in thick gusts. The van lay in a small hollow maybe fifty feet from the road. It had left a path of scrunched snow behind. Undoubtedly the snow had cushioned the impact. On the road I saw the back-up traffic at the original accident, a station wagon across two lanes of traffic, one tire at the horizontal. A jackknifed semi-trailer rested in the highway median strip. I turned back to the van. No one moved inside. We managed the untying clumsily. With me leaning on Monica's arm and proceeding slowly, we made our way toward the highway. Several figures hurried down the slope toward us.

Eventually I wound up on the passenger side of one of the cars caught in the jam. The driver, a teenage boy chewing gum at a machine-gun rate, kept the motor running. They'd wrapped extra blankets around me. The comforting warmth soon put me to sleep. I woke to movement.

Out the front window I saw the back of an enormous snowplow. "Are you all right?" Monica's voice asked from behind me. A comforting hand appeared on my shoulder.

"Okay, I guess," I mumbled.

"Ambulances can't get through," she explained. I lost the rest of what she said in a pain-soaked doze.

What felt like hours later, at a hospital that seemed to loom out of a vast snowfield, someone finally jammed some pain-killer into me. The doctor said they didn't need to keep me. They don't even tape broken ribs any more. He told me to take it easy, rest a lot, and use the pain pills.

Monica and I sat on a couch outside the emergency room waiting for Scott to come pick us up. Others from the various wrecks had been brought in with us, plus some people stranded in the storm. Monica had gotten the local police involved and called Chicago. Scott and Jerry were safe. Around two in the afternoon the storm let up. At four I took a couple of pain pills. Shortly after five Scott drove up in my truck.

Heads turned as he walked toward us. He hugged me gently and tenderly.

The cab of the truck held the three of us comfortably. "Any problems getting here?" I asked, watching the moonlight shine on the crisp, untrodden snow in the fields next to the road.

He patted the dashboard. "Your magic machine can go through anything. I stopped a few times to help people; otherwise no problem." He maneuvered the truck carefully around a family of five creeping down the half-cleared highway. "The Chicago cop, Paul Turner, wants to see us."

Monica and I told Scott all that happened and all Priscilla had confessed to. The last word I had in the hospital was that one of the women was dead; Stephanie was in intensive care, given a fifty-fifty chance of survival; Priscilla was well enough to be questioned; they were still operating on Sally.

Two hours later I lay on a couch in Scott's living room. I'd showered but not shaved. Scott suggested I not do so. The blue shadow of a day's neglected growth of my beard turns him on.

We dined on cans of soup and garlic bread thawed in the microwave. Afterward he sat on the floor by the couch I lay on. He held my hand and caressed my arm. We were waiting for Turner.

On the way back from the hospital he'd told me what happened to him and Jerry. He'd stumbled to the room with the gaping hole in the floor. He'd leaped the opening, one foot landing safely, the other scraping on the edge. He had enough time to pull himself into a far corner, half-hidden by scaffolding and paint cans. Seconds later they'd flashed a light on the hole in the floor and quickly moved on. For many minutes Scott heard the frantic searching and internecine fighting. Silence followed. He waited, crazy with worry, for the two of us. Finally he heard stealthy creeping outside. A shadow appeared at the door. He didn't think the searchers would come alone. He called Jerry's name very softly. The boy almost rushed into the room. Scott stopped him in time, leaped into the corridor, and led the way to the exit. At the window they saw the van pulling away. They'd gotten out and called the police. Because of the snow, Glen and Jeannette had to take the train in from River's Edge to get Jerry. Public transportation was the only thing running in the area at the time. Hours later, when he got Monica's call from the hospital, the roads had been cleared enough for him to drive out.

Turner came by at eight-fifteen. I sat up on the couch, the

pain masked by a pill. He sat down alongside me. He wore a heavy winter coat over a three-piece suit. Most of the stuff I told him, he knew already from Scott, Jerry, and Monica. I talked about Priscilla's confession.

"I'll never understand people like that," I said

"Desperate people pushed beyond their limits," Scott said, shrugging. "They're capable of anything."

Turner had remained quiet during my story, asking only an occasional question. When I finished, he got up off the couch and walked to the far end of the room. From the west window he gazed out at the snow-blanketed city. He turned back to us, hands in the pockets of his suit pants, and walked halfway across the room. He stopped at the trophy table and touched each one with the tips of his fingers.

The only lights on in the room were two table lamps on either side of the couch. The light shone on his somber face. He was around five nine and heavily muscled, a wrestler or body builder rather than a swimmer. He smiled at the two of us. Scott was sitting on the couch next to me, our knees touching.

"They didn't kill him," he said.

We did shocked "Uh? What?"s.

"It took some doing, but I tracked down the guy who did the toxicology report on Sebastian. He was scared, and he didn't tell me all, but I got enough."

He strode over and sat on the white overstuffed couch facing us. "That crowd tried to poison him all right, but like most things Priscilla and the Lesbian Radicals from Hell did, it was ill planned, poorly executed, and half baked from the beginning. They managed to be politically correct but horribly stupid. Prentice opened a new bottle of wine and put poison in it, but Sebastian used wine from an already opened bottle."

"How'd he die?" Scott asked.

"He never drank arsenic. None showed up in his system. Somebody else put cyanide in something Sebastian ate or drank. That's what killed him."

"Couldn't Priscilla and Prentice have used both poisons?"

"I got a report just before I came over here from the cop who questioned Priscilla. She never mentioned cyanide. When the cop asked, she denied it. The cop believes her. She had no reason to lie to you and Monica in the car. For the moment we have no proof they did. We're questioning everybody again. Those precious housekeepers would be in the city by now being interrogated if the snow hadn't screwed things up. The River's Edge cops are bringing them in. They prepared all his meals for the past ten years. I'm going over now. You can come along, but I ask the questions."

Mildred and Harriet Weber seemed glad to see us, while expressing fascinated interest in the nice young men around them. They didn't seem in the least put out, bothered, or afraid. We stayed for the first half hour of questioning. They insisted they didn't want a lawyer, twittered and nodded together in their usual fashion. Turner showed remarkable patience. He soon had them chattering away to him like old friends. We stepped out and drank a cup of coffee provided by one of the detectives. We talked baseball with him and two men who came in from duty.

Turner came out of the room shaking his head. He beckoned us over. "If they did it, they're better than any street member or hardened creep I've ever met. Everything they say sounds right. Practically rehearsed, it's so good. My instinct tells me they're innocent. We'll question them a while longer. We've got men from the River's Edge police department searching their house and the rectory." He twisted his neck, rolled his head in an exercise loop, then shrugged. "Maybe Priscilla and her pals screwed it up and accidentally poisoned him correctly."

We expected Scott's parents the next day, and we had a few last-minute preparations. I also felt the need for a pain pill coming on. In bed Scott held me gently for the longest time. I fell asleep in his arms.

I awoke once in the night to take another pill. Returning from the kitchen, I stood over the bed, watching him sleep. In our king-size bed he lay on his side facing me. The famous right arm reached toward the empty spot I'd soon fill. He slept deeply. I crawled in and snuggled close to his warmth. I lay awake waiting for the pill to take effect, wondering who killed the only good priest.

I woke stiff and sore around ten the next morning. Scott insisted I stay in bed. I took a pill, got up, and surrendered myself to a half-hour shower as hot as I could stand it. He has a gay cleaning service in once a week. He'd hired them for an extra few hours this week to make sure things were perfect for his parents.

I haven't cleaned for my parents in years. Of course, we see them all the time. My mother never mentions the dust or the fact that the kitchen floor usually needs scrubbing. She figures it's my mess and doesn't care as long as she doesn't have to live with it. Scott is more fastidious. I'm pretty careful at his place, cleaning up after myself. I have one small room as a sort of den that I slob around in. Even this I cleaned today. He used to nag me about cleaning my house. The last time he nagged seven years ago, I got him a rag, sponge, dust mop, and pail. Told him if it bothered him so much, he was welcome to take care of it. We got pretty steamed at each other that night, but we reached a compromise that has lasted all these years.

Scott's Porsche and my truck were both too small for airport pickup duty. Scott hired a limousine to bring his parents to his place. We'd meet on our turf.

During the day, Paul Turner called to say the searchers had found nothing at Mildred and Harriet's or at the rectory. He also said that Stephanie and Sally would live, and that they'd arrested Prentice. They'd let Mildred and Harriet go. I fielded calls from Monica and Neil expressing concern, from Glen bubbling with thanks, and from Kurt announcing a settlement of the contract at school.

Scott's parents turned out to be fun. His father was as tall as Scott but thinner, slightly bald, with bright red cheeks and large hands. His mother might have been all of five feet tall. She hugged him fiercely and gave me a tentative smile. His dad shook my hand, seemed surprised I didn't crumble under a handshake I think he meant to be bone crushing. His dad spent the first half hour inspecting Scott's trophies. Scott only keeps out a few. When dad insisted, Scott dragged out all the others from a storeroom deep in the penthouse.

Unknown to me, Scott also dragged out my high school trophies. I'd forgotten they were here. After seeing my senior year all-state fullback trophy, Mr. Carpenter found it hard to keep from beaming at me. If I was an athlete, I couldn't be all bad. Usually, I resent it when my sports background makes my being gay acceptable to relentlessly straight people like Mr. Carpenter. However, one must learn to put up with a great deal from one's in-laws.

For dinner Mr. Carpenter wanted a good Chicago piece of beef. We took them to Lawry's–The Prime Rib. He ate the Chicago cut, devouring all the sumptuous food in great gulps. Mrs. Carpenter oohed and aahed over the sites as we drove to the restaurant. She beamed with pride whenever somebody asked for Scott's autograph and every time we caught the whisper of "There's Scott Carpenter!" She barely touched her food.

Scott's dad loosened up enough to tell tales of Scott growing up. Baseball games and childhood mischief, learning to fix things, keeping watch for intruders at the old still, their first trip together to Atlanta to watch a Braves game, Scott vowing to be a pitcher when he grew up.

"And my boy grew up to do just that." He slapped Scott on the back with obvious pride in his accomplishment.

I tried discreetly to pop a pain pill with my coffee after the meal, but Mrs. Carpenter caught the movement and asked what was wrong. Scott explained our adventures, giving them an edited version. After all, this was a family show. Mrs. Carpenter clucked sympathetically.

We dropped them at the door of the Hyatt Regency on Wacker Drive. Scott'd hired the limousine for the duration of their stay. Tomorrow he'd use it to take them around town.

As we climbed out of our dress suits in the bedroom, I said, "I like your parents. I don't think your dad views me as an alien out to destroy his son, although I don't think we're ready to be best friends either. Your mom is nice, sweet. Did you really do all those things your dad said when you were a kid?"

I sat on my side of the bed in my Jockey shorts.

"Yes," he mumbled from the closet.

I slipped my shorts off and sank into the comfortable bed. It was only ten, so I picked up the book I'd been reading from the nightstand, *The Company We Keep*. I pulled the covers up. He emerged naked from the closet and picked various pieces of clothing off the floor, depositing them in the proper receptacles. I admired the fluid grace of his muscles as he accomplished these mundane tasks. I felt the first stirrings of desire. He crawled into bed, turned off his light, and moved close to me.

"You really kept watch at your dad's still?" I asked.

He laughed. "Only until I was six. The hollow we kept it in flooded that year and washed it all away. Wasn't worth rebuilding. I used to help him out, fix the tubing, pour in the ingredients, help him bottle it. We even had this contraption to switch ingredients to get them in exact proportions. It never really worked very well."

I moved away and turned on the light.

"What?" Scott said.

"That's the solution: switching ingredients! Was Sebastian taking AZT or anything else because he was HIV positive? Who knew he had AIDS and took medicine, and who had access to it?"

He shrugged. "The police probably checked for all that stuff as a routine."

"No, they didn't. Remember what Turner said? If they did get reports, they didn't follow up. Who knew he had AIDS?"

Scott sighed. He lay back on his pillow. "Neil, Monica, and Brian Clayton claimed they didn't know."

"Priscilla and Prentice acted surprised at the news. The Weber sisters didn't say anything about it."

"The therapist knew," Scott said.

"Smith knew," I said. "I'd bet the rent that smug shit at the chancery killed him. I'd bet the penthouse I'm right."

He rolled on his side and looked at me. "The priest did it?"

"Yep."

"Why?"

"Don't know yet." In my excitement I'd forgotten my painful ribs. I twisted quickly to get up. A sharp jolt brought me up short.

"Easy," Scott said. "I think he's a shit, but that doesn't mean he committed murder."

"He's a shit *and* a murderer." I got up. "We're going over there now."

"Shouldn't we call Turner in the morning? You have no proof he even had access to any medicine. Others must have known. Come back to bed."

"Very few people knew. Sebastian was real close-mouthed. I want to do something about it now." I began to get dressed. With some reluctance he followed suit.

Outside, the cold snap that normally follows snow in Chicago in winter had arrived on schedule. We took a cab to the cathedral rectory, arriving just after ten forty-five. "They're probably all asleep," he mumbled as we drove over. The place blazed with light. A fairly drunk priest opened the door. He cast a more than appreciative glance at us as we stood in the hallway. I couldn't imagine how gay priests could live with themselves and speak for a church that feared and hated them. He swished his pudgy form up a flight of stairs and returned with Bishop Smith, then left. Smith wore his black pants, suit jacket, and Roman collar. He'd drunk far less than his recently departed brother of the cloth.

He ushered us into the study and offered us a drink. We said no.

"It's late for a social call, gentlemen. I'd like to get back to the party upstairs."

"You're the murderer," I said. As I explained, the priest's gray eyebrows gathered in a condescending frown.

"That's absurd," he said when I finished. He stood up. "I'll thank you to leave."

"We're staying," I said. "You could have tampered with his medicine at any time, maybe on a visit to the rectory. Who would be suspicious of a bishop?"

"I'll make allowances for the trauma you've been through," Smith said. "However, you are beginning to try my patience."

I said, "Tomorrow morning we'll see who else knew about the medicine. Somebody must have what was left of his pills. We'll find out who in the police department had them, or is supposed to have them. We'll find a trail that leads to you."

He laughed. "You boys had best take your vivid imaginations and go."

Eventually Scott led me out, sputtering and defiant.

"He did it," I kept repeating as we took a cab home.

"We can't prove it," Scott said.

"Drive to the Twenty-third District police station, Clark and Addison," I ordered the cab driver.

"Now what?" Scott asked. "It's late. You're still recovering from the accident. You need rest."

"I want to know who's got the medicine now, and who knew he was taking it." To the police station, up the stairs from Halsted Street, through the door, to the front desk, where we asked for Turner. He wasn't in. The cops recognized Scott and offered to help us. One cop said somebody else had called for Turner only a few minutes before.

"Smith," I guessed.

"I could tell you from the central computer downtown tomorrow," the cop said. We described Smith's voice, but he wasn't sure it was the same one.

I asked about tracing the medicine. It was late, but for Scott Carpenter, they'd do what they could. After fifteen minutes of phone calls a cop came back to us.

"I had somebody in the evidence lockup check the records in the case. No pills or medicine checked in at any point."

I was on my way out the door. I heard Scott thank the cop for his help. Slowed by my ribs, I eased toward the curb. I wanted a pain pill. I hailed a cab. Scott joined me.

"You're going to have to slow down," Scott said. "We have no proof there were any pills. You're convinced it's the priest. It could be any number of people. Let's go home."

I said, "One more stop: Roscoe's. Let's see if we can't get the bartender to identify the therapist and Bishop Smith."

"What for?" Scott asked.

"Humor me, please."

He shrugged agreement.

We found the bartender who'd recognized Sebastian's picture. An unusually large crowd and loud noise from the videos made it difficult for us to talk to him. Finally, Scott pulled him aside near the back of the bar. I leaned close enough to hear. Scott gave him two descriptions, one of Smith, the other of the psychologist Kramer.

The bartender shrugged. "Could be either guy. Even if I saw them together, I doubt I'd be sure. In fact it could have been both of them, now that you mention it, on the same night in here. Lots of people stopped by to talk to the priest because he wore the outfit." Several patrons tried to get his attention. "Look, I got to get back. Sorry."

"What did that prove?" Scott asked.

"It establishes a point of contact," I said.

"Don't take this wrong," Scott said, "but big fucking deal. You're being stubborn and not looking at this logically."

"I don't care." I felt unreasonable and put upon. "I'm going out to the rectory to look for those pills. You don't know for sure they aren't there."

He slammed his fist down on the bar. Nearby patrons stared. A few moved away. "Will you stop and think?" he demanded. "You want to go running around the city and suburbs on some wild chase after what very likely doesn't exist?"

I stared into those deep blue eyes. He put a hand on my arm. "Think," he said calmly.

I turned and placed my elbows on the bar. He moved close and placed an arm gently around my shoulders. I could feel the warmth of his closeness.

"It's late," he said. "We can talk about this more quietly at home."

"I guess." As we turned to go, I grabbed his sleeve. "Monica's source, the old guy, Father Stuart!" I said.

"Now what?"

"The Weber sisters said he'd been one of the ones who came to clear out Sebastian's room at the rectory."

"The old guy didn't do it," Scott said.

We bickered and argued out the door and in the cab, all the way back to the cathedral rectory. The lecherous drunk at the door told us where Father Stuart's room was. The sounds of a party still echoed on the second floor. Up on the third floor we marched to Stuart's room. Light came from under the door, but I got no answer to my knock. I opened the door. Smith sat on the bed with his head in his hands. Stuart sat at a desk, a dark brown prescription bottle in front of him.

"I've been expecting you gentlemen," Stuart said.

We sat down in chairs opposite the bed. The room had a large oriental rug in the center, with polished hardwood around the edges. A window looked out onto State Street. On one wall Stuart had a collection of Victorian miniature paintings, all elegantly framed. Other than a cross over the head of the bed, these were the only decorations. Only one light was on in the room. The lamp on the desk shone on Stuart's hands on the desk and on his eyes.

Silence built for several minutes.

"Why?" I asked.

Smith pulled his hands away from his head. He stared at the tips of the fingernails on his right hand while he spoke. "We were so close when we were in seminary. A year ago I'd begun meeting him every Sunday to talk over the life we had. I'd watched his career. He'd become a dedicated, brave man, defying the diocese and not hiding his homosexuality. I'd finally learned how much I needed love. In the seminary I rejected his advances. I'd let him hug me chastely. He wanted passion. I wouldn't respond. I was terrified. I almost turned him in. I'd have ruined a good priest's life." He sighed. "I'll never forget that time we flew to Selma together."

180

"Father Stuart told us about it," I said.

He finally looked up. "Probably not everything. We went to Selma to march. I took one look at the situation and got on the next plane back to Chicago. He stayed. He cared. He had commitment and drive. He deserved the honors and placement that were coming to me.

"I wanted his love. I told him so. I told him that after all these years I loved him." He drew a shuddering breath. "He rejected me, very kindly, very gently. He said I'd have to find my own person to love. Then he told me he had AIDS."

A tear formed at the corner of his eye and began to trickle down his cheek. "I'd gotten everything I'd ever wanted in my life. I'm clever and competent, and I became a very powerful bishop. Now I realized the one thing I wanted more than anything else was his love and respect. I saw I'd never have either. I also felt incredible guilt. If I'd loved him all those years ago, he wouldn't be dying. I wanted to hurt him."

He took out a hankerchief and wiped his face. He continued dry-eyed. "God, how I hated him! I wanted to kill him. Who knew when he'd die from an opportunistic infection? I began trying to poison him. I tried it a few times with his drinks at Roscoe's, but the opportunity never came up. If nothing else, that damn therapist was in the way. Sebastian told me he was taking AZT. I figured that was my chance. I visited the rectory numerous times. On one of my visits I went to his room. I emptied the medicine from two of the capsules and substituted cyanide. I wasn't sure of the amount needed. I didn't know when he'd take the fatal dose. Eventually he did, and he died. After your visit tonight, I figured I had to get the rest of the medicine back, to see if there were any traces or if the second capsule was left. I came here to ask Father Stuart. I knew he had helped clean the room. Now you know everything."

Saturday afternoon I talked to Kramer the therapist. He unbent far enough to tell me that Sebastian had come to him after he tested positive. Sebastian had broken his vow of celibacy once, six years ago. The guilt and self-recriminations had nearly driven him crazy. As far as Kramer knew, Sebastian had told only Smith about having AIDS, so my guess the night before had been accurate. Only Smith could have known to sabotage his medicine.

On Saturday evening at my place, Glen, Scott, Jerry, and I were eating popcorn and playing Monopoly, as usual.

"You should've seen 'em, Dad," he said for the tenth time. "Uncle Tom and Uncle Scott were great. They could fight a battalion by themselves." Such is the faith of twelve-year-olds.

In the kitchen earlier I asked Glen how the kid had been. "Scared but okay," he told me. They'd gone to a therapist as a family. He'd told them to come back only if Jerry showed signs of having problems.

Later, Jerry came in the kitchen while I stacked dirty dishes. Glen and Scott cleaned up the living room.

"We haven't had much time to talk," I said. "How're you holding up? That must have been awful to go through." I'd gotten sketchy details of the ordeal from Glen. Jerry talked about it for a little bit, seemed uneasy. Finally he blurted out, "What if you guys hadn't shown up?"

I put an arm on his shoulder and he moved into an embrace. Another year or so and he wouldn't want an adult near him.

I held him, soothed him. Scott called from the living room. "Jerry, your dad's in the car waiting."

Jerry looked up at me and said, "I love you, Uncle Tom."

"I love you too," I said. With a final squeeze he bounced out of the kitchen. I joined Scott in the living room. As we stood together and watched their car's taillights move out of the driveway and pull away, I put my arm around Scott's waist and pulled him close.